THE ADVENTURES OF
THE BAILEY
SCHOOL KIDS®
GHOSTS DON'T EAT
POTATO CHIPS

A GRAPHIC NOVEL BY ANGELI RAFER

BASED ON THE NOVEL BY
MARCIA THORNTON JONES & DEBBIE DADEY
WITH COLOR BY **WES DZIOBA**

graphix

An Imprint of
■SCHOLASTIC

TO MY FELINE FAMILY MEMBERS, PAST AND PRESENT, WHO PURRED THEIR WAY INTO MY HOME AND HEART: SASHA, KRYSTAL, TAZZ, PURRL, CALLIOPE, COCO-MO, GEMMA, AND IZZY! — MARCIA THORNTON JONES

FOR ALEX — DEBBIE DADEY

FOR MOM, DAD, KUYA LORENZO, AND TITA ROWIE — AND YOU, THE READER, WHO PICKED UP THIS GRAPHIC NOVEL. MAY YOU ALWAYS GET LOST IN A GOOD BOOK; MAY YOU STAY HUNGRY FOR MORE! — ANGELI RAFER

Text copyright © 1992, 2023 by Marcia Thornton Jones and Debra S. Dadey
Art copyright © 2023 by Angeli Rafer

Some character and setting illustrations are either based on or inspired by character and setting depictions originally designed by Pearl Low.

Library of Congress Control Number: 2022946124

ISBN 978-1-338-88166-0 (hardcover)
ISBN 978-1-338-88165-3 (paperback)

10 9 8 7 6 5 4 3 2 1   23 24 25 26 27

Printed in China   62
First edition, September 2023

Edited by Jonah Newman
Book design by Steve Ponzo and Shivana Sookdeo
Color flatting by Aaron Polk
Creative Director: Phil Falco
Publisher: David Saylor

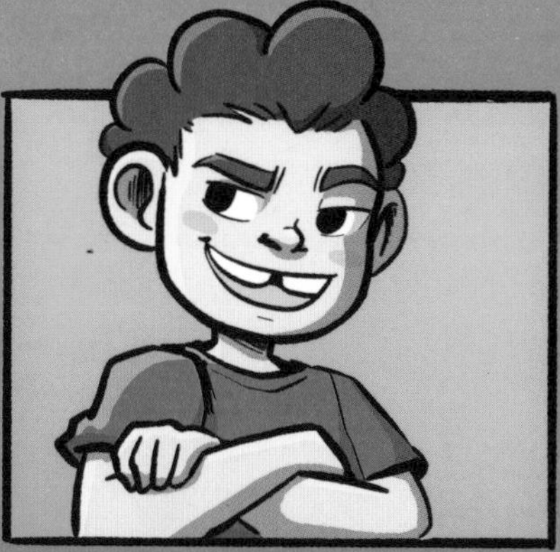

EDDIE

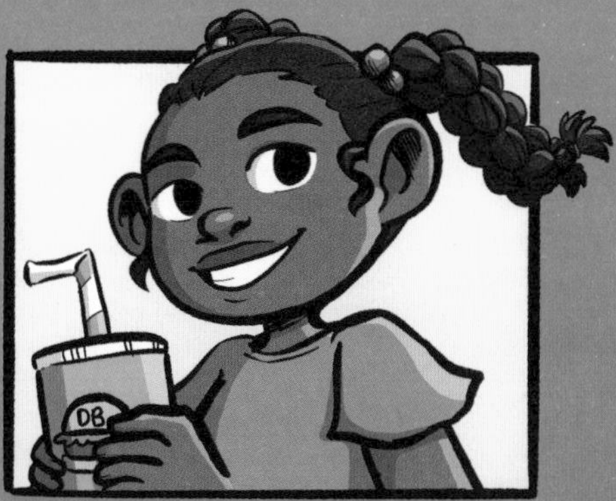
DB

MELODY

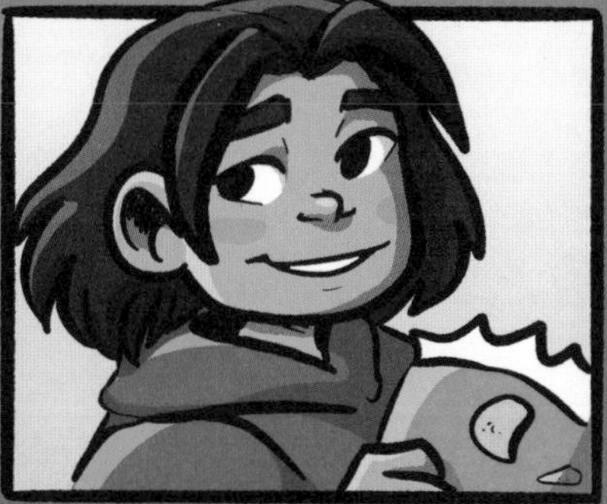

HOWIE

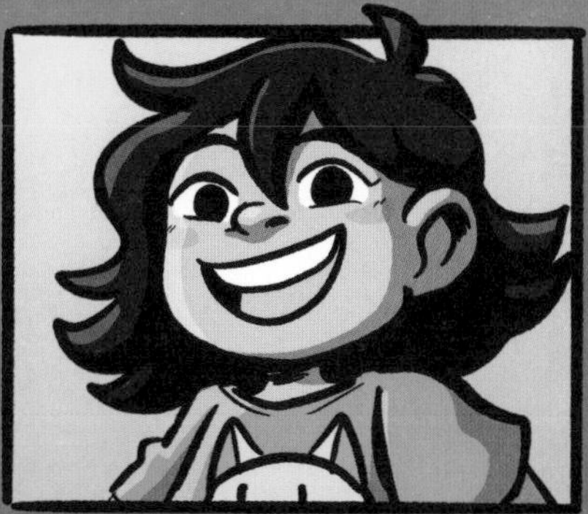

LIZA

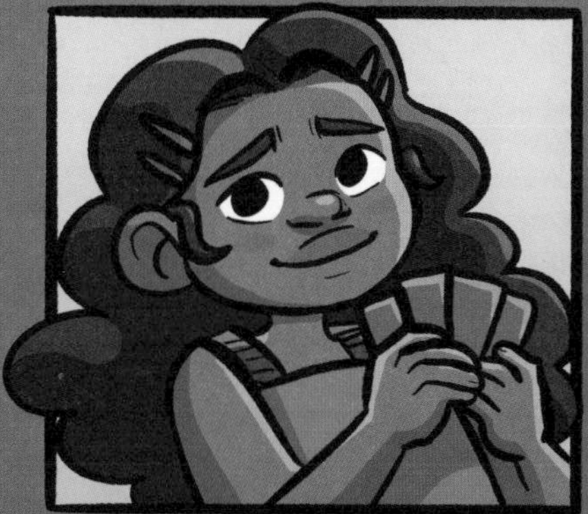

CAREY

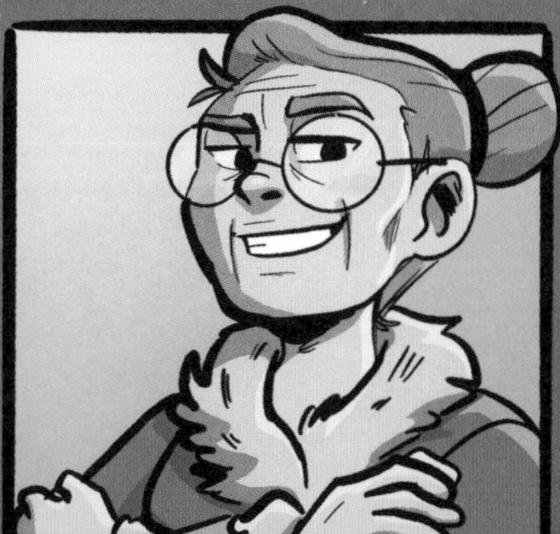

GREAT-AUNT MATHILDA

GREAT-UNCLE JASPER

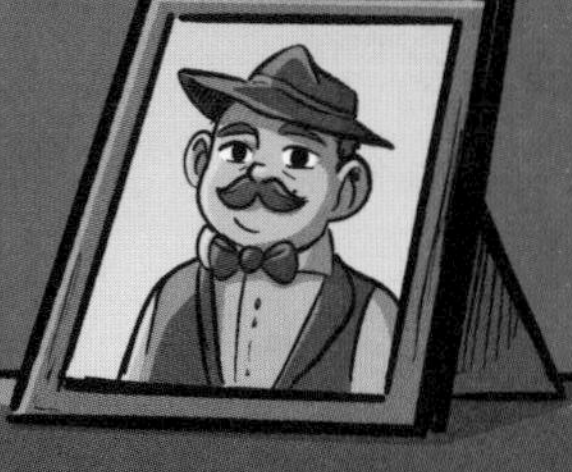

CHAPTER 1 GREAT-AUNT MATHILDA

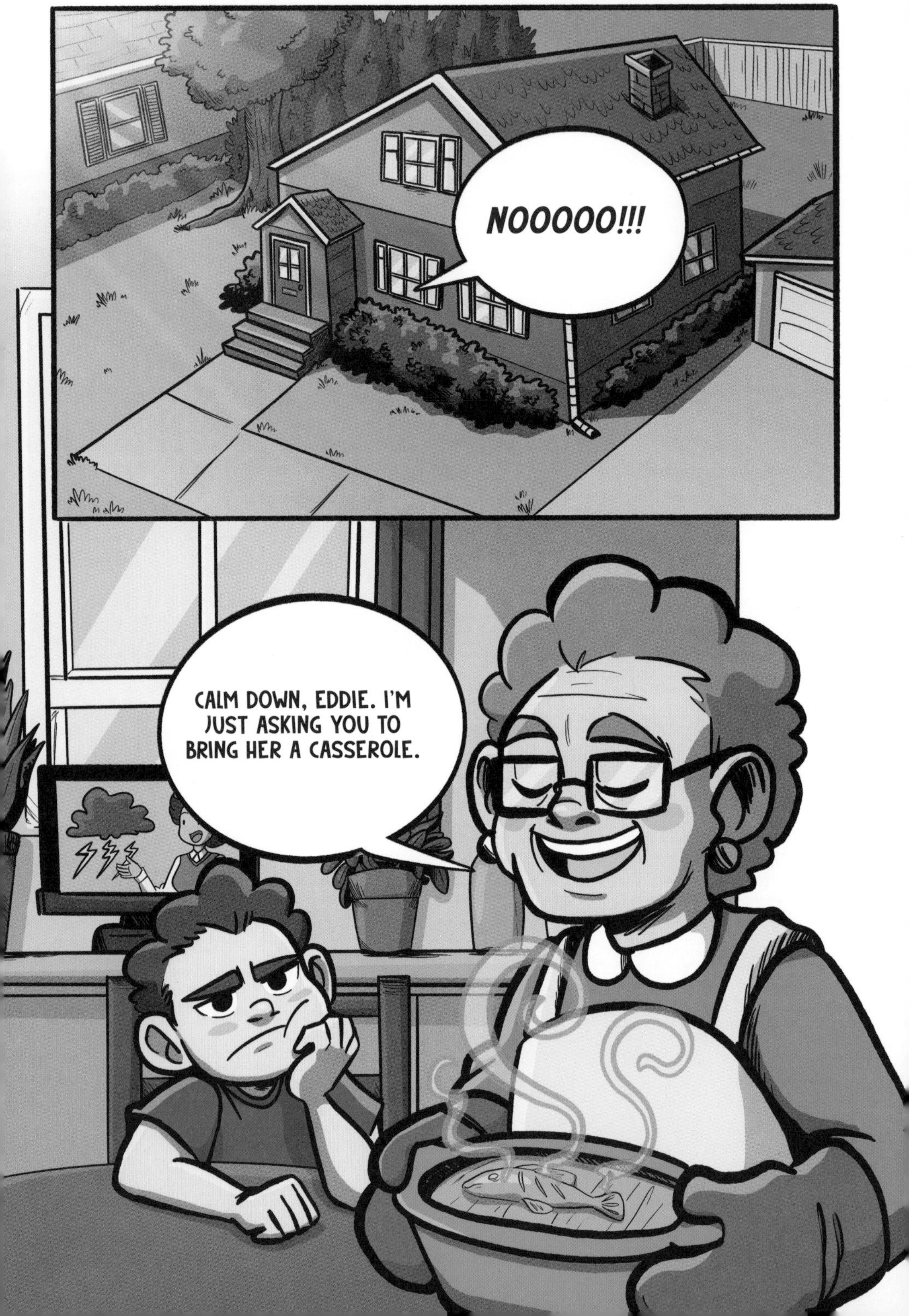
NOOOOO!!!
CALM DOWN, EDDIE. I'M JUST ASKING YOU TO BRING HER A CASSEROLE.

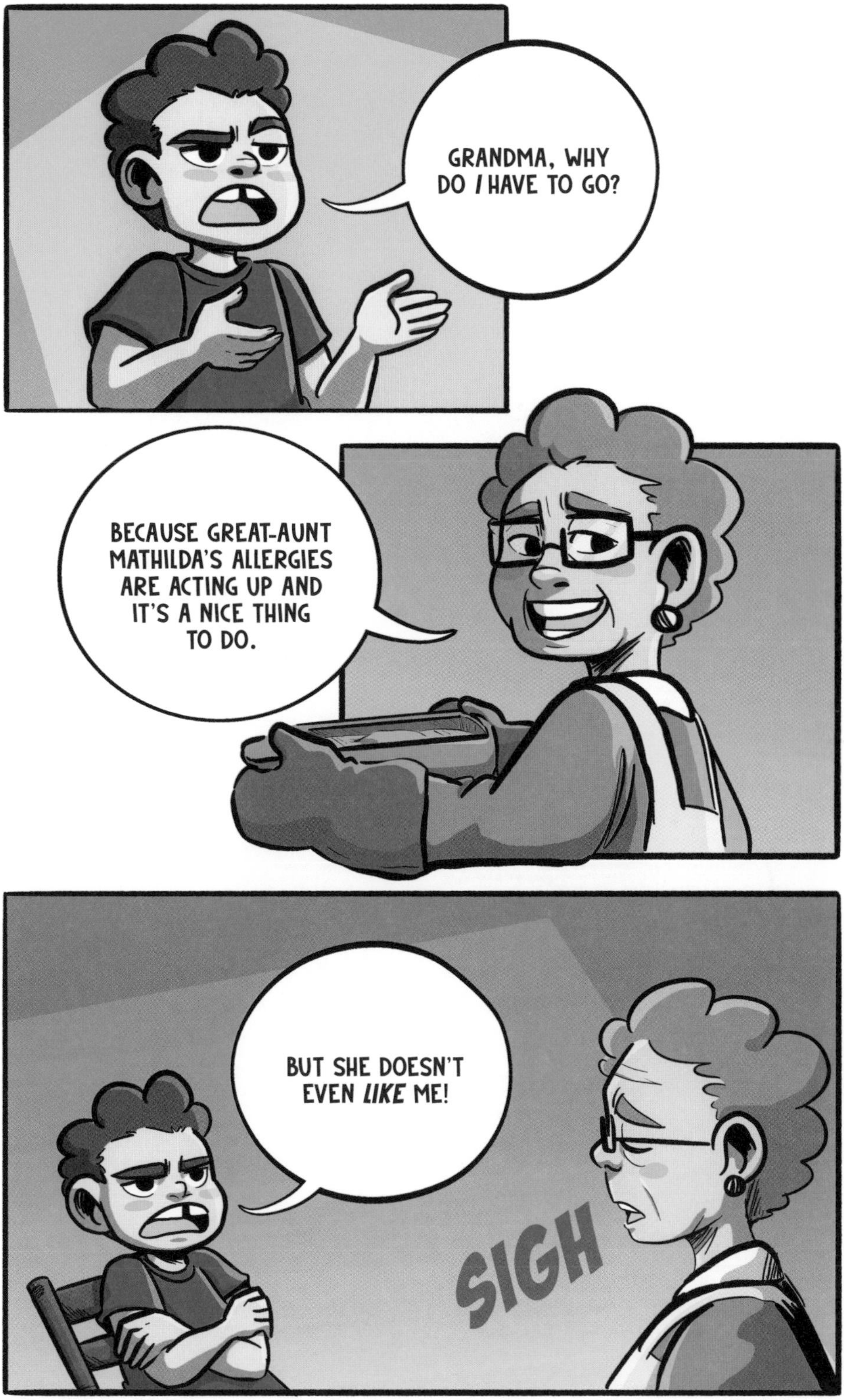
GRANDMA, WHY DO *I* HAVE TO GO?
BECAUSE GREAT-AUNT MATHILDA'S ALLERGIES ARE ACTING UP AND IT'S A NICE THING TO DO.
BUT SHE DOESN'T EVEN *LIKE* ME!
SIGH

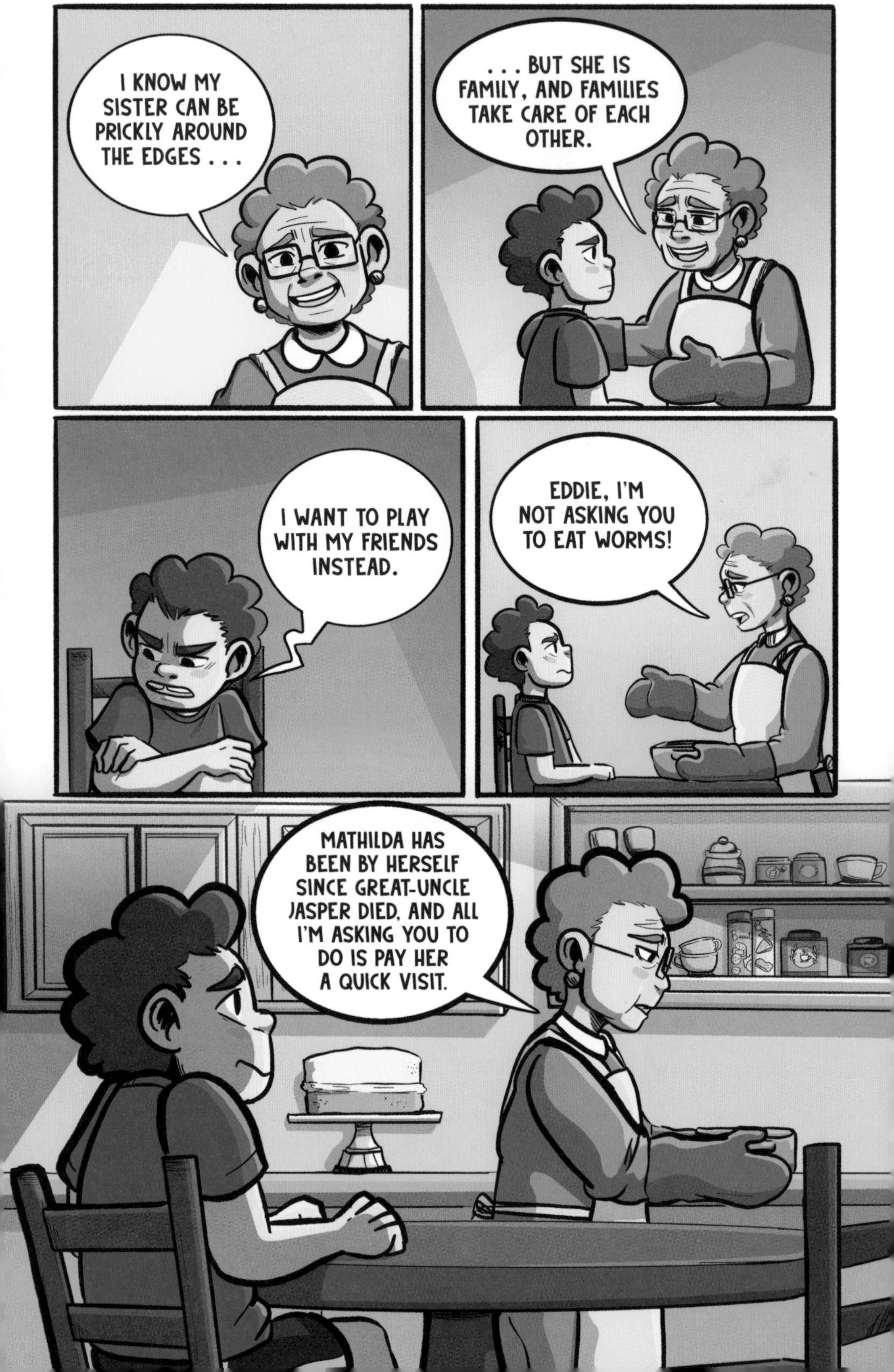
I KNOW MY SISTER CAN BE PRICKLY AROUND THE EDGES . . .
. . . BUT SHE IS FAMILY, AND FAMILIES TAKE CARE OF EACH OTHER.
I WANT TO PLAY WITH MY FRIENDS INSTEAD.
EDDIE, I'M NOT ASKING YOU TO EAT WORMS!
MATHILDA HAS BEEN BY HERSELF SINCE GREAT-UNCLE JASPER DIED, AND ALL I'M ASKING YOU TO DO IS PAY HER A QUICK VISIT.

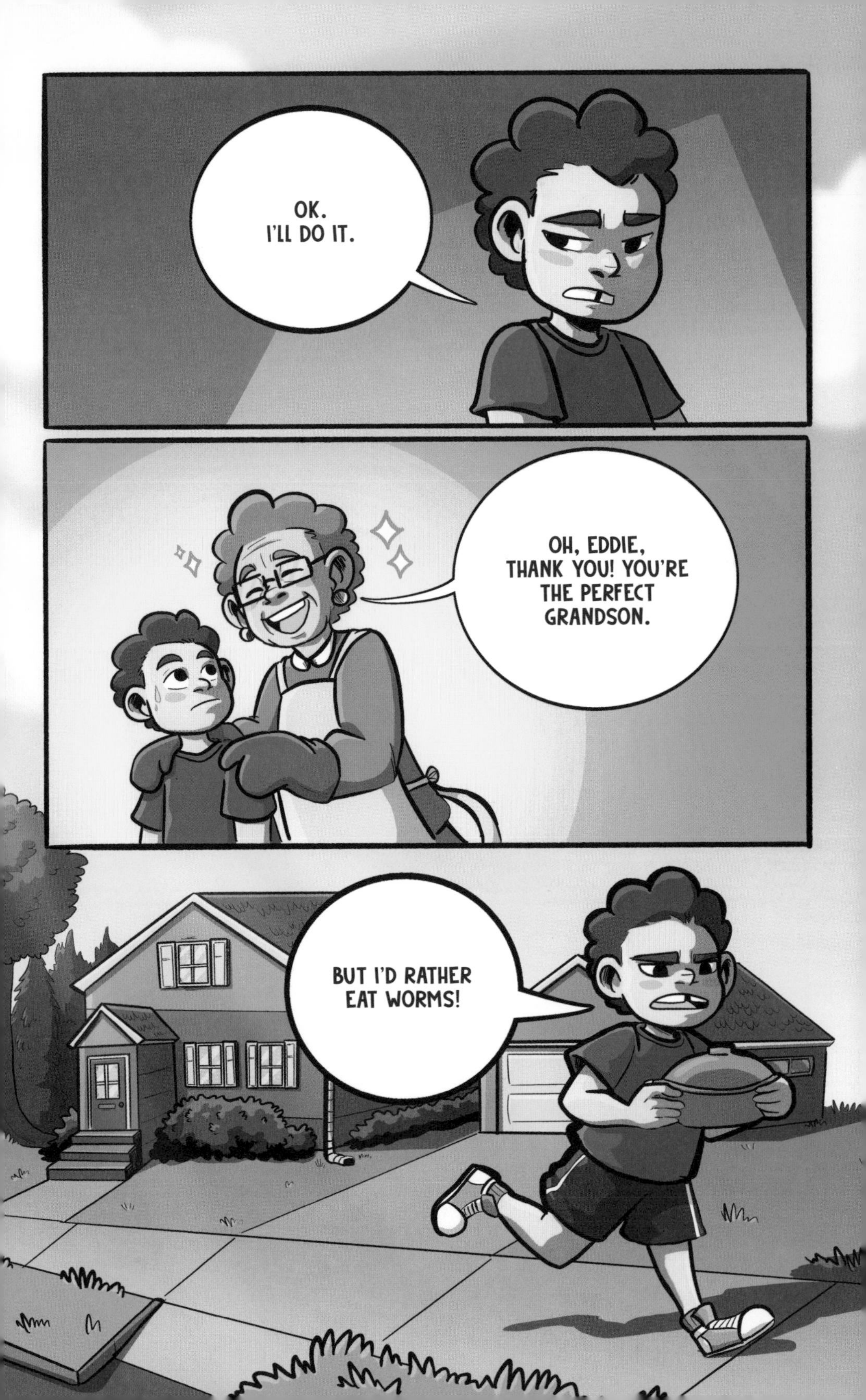
OK. I'LL DO IT.
OH, EDDIE, THANK YOU! YOU'RE THE PERFECT GRANDSON.
BUT I'D RATHER EAT WORMS!

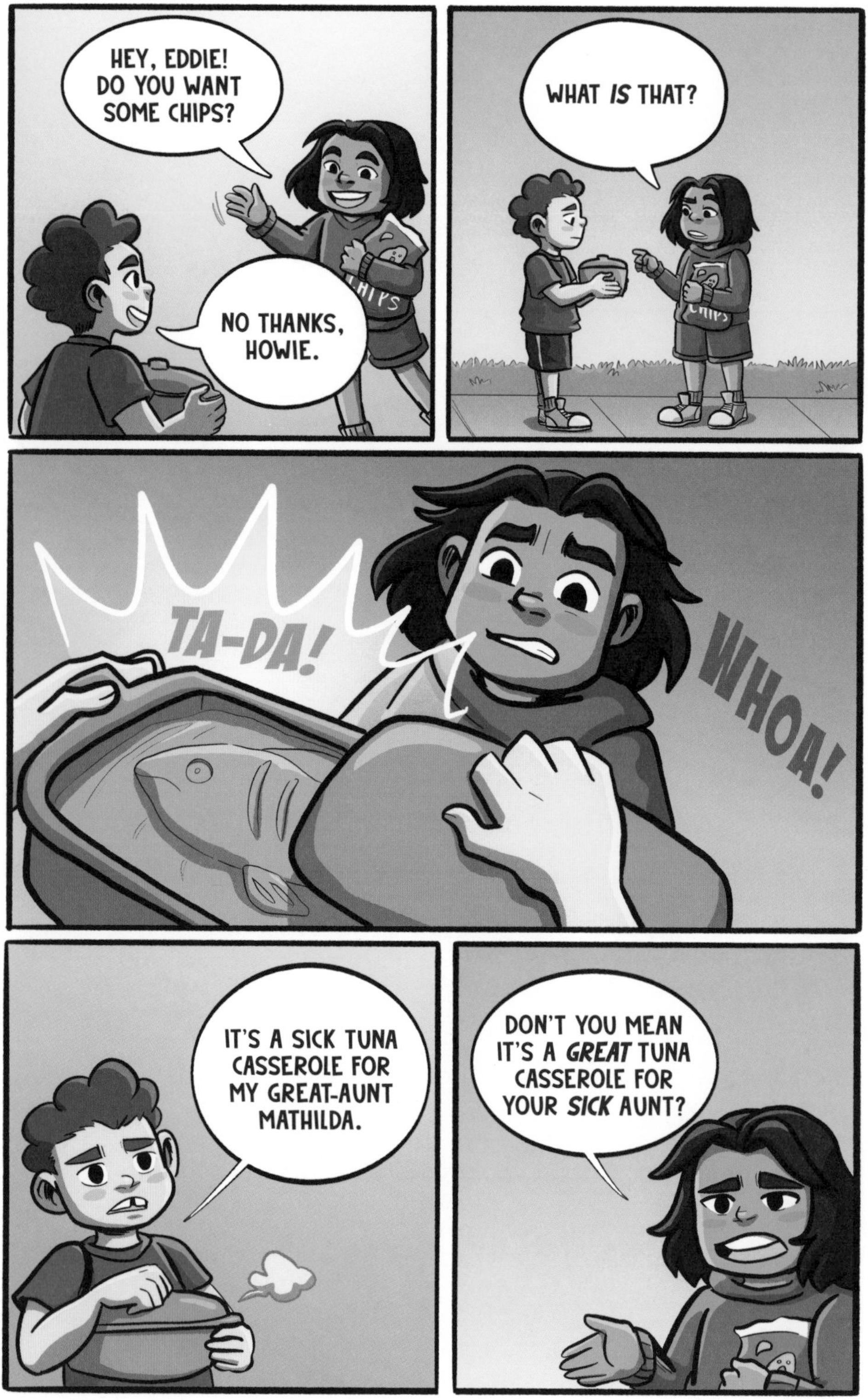
HEY, EDDIE! DO YOU WANT SOME CHIPS?
CHIPS
NO THANKS, HOWIE.
WHAT *IS* THAT?
TA-DA!
WHOA!
IT'S A SICK TUNA CASSEROLE FOR MY GREAT-AUNT MATHILDA.
DON'T YOU MEAN IT'S A *GREAT* TUNA CASSEROLE FOR YOUR *SICK* AUNT?

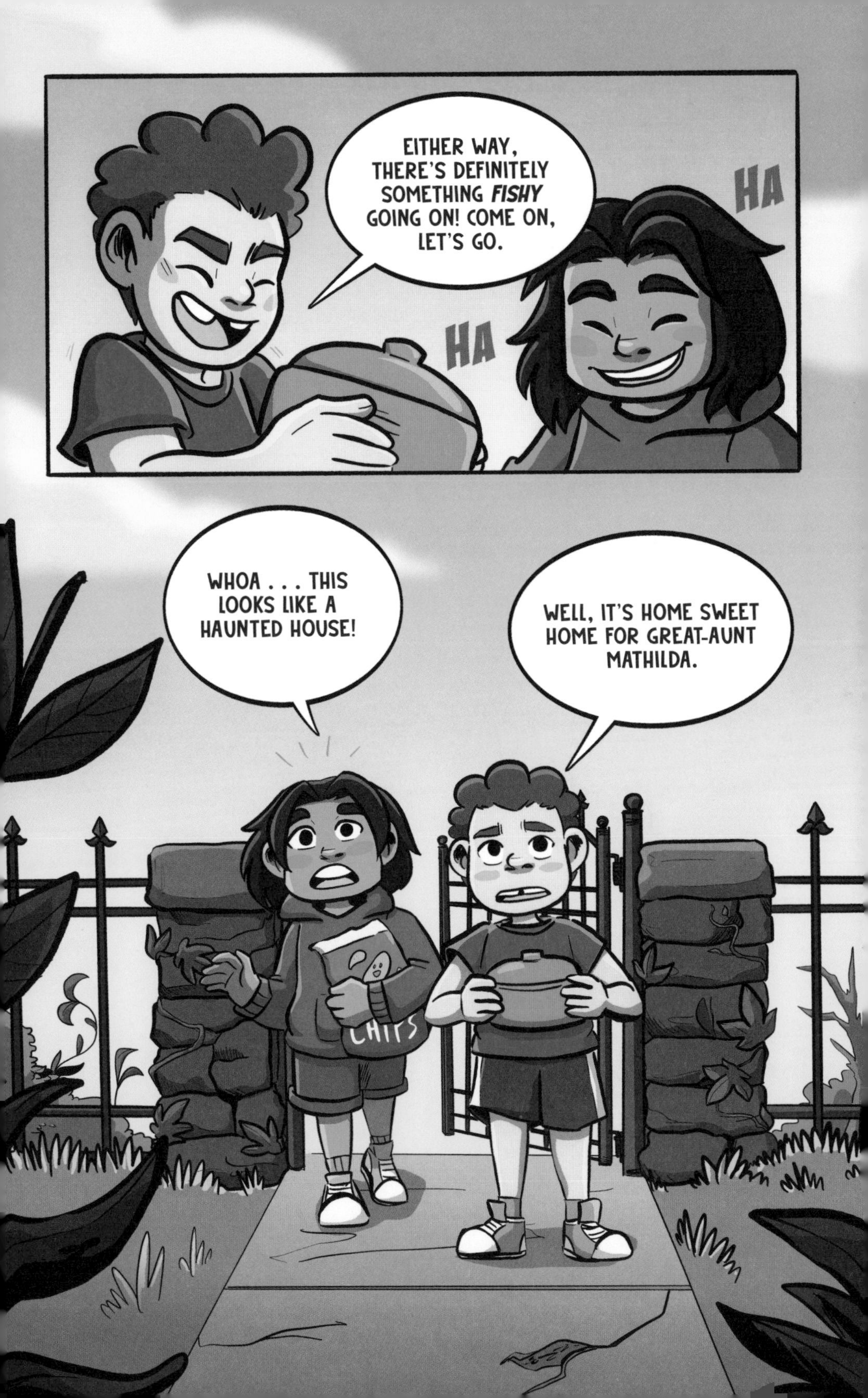
EITHER WAY, THERE'S DEFINITELY SOMETHING *FISHY* GOING ON! COME ON, LET'S GO.
HA
HA
WHOA . . . THIS LOOKS LIKE A HAUNTED HOUSE!
WELL, IT'S HOME SWEET HOME FOR GREAT-AUNT MATHILDA.
CHIPS

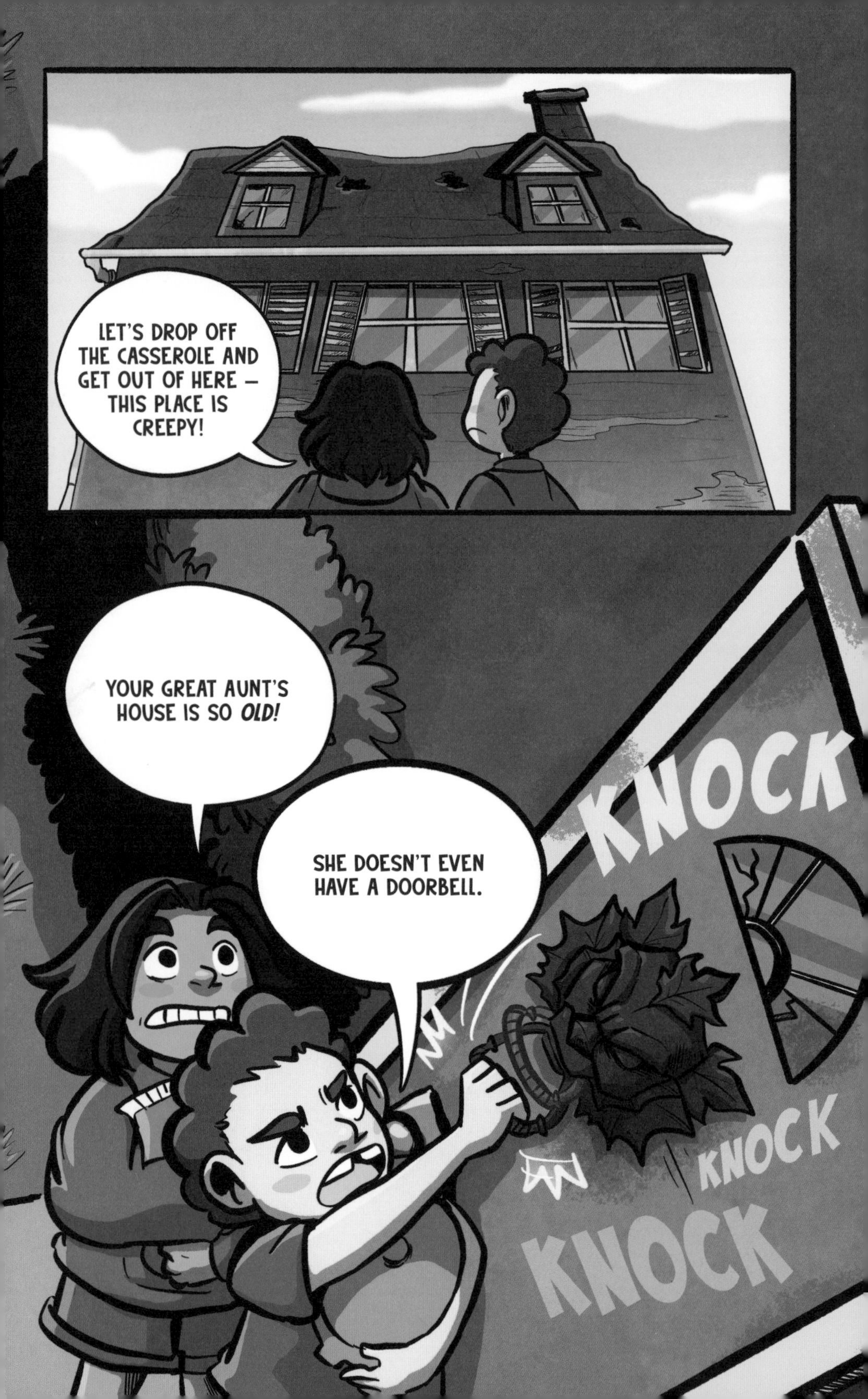
LET'S DROP OFF THE CASSEROLE AND GET OUT OF HERE — THIS PLACE IS CREEPY!
YOUR GREAT AUNT'S HOUSE IS SO *OLD!*
SHE DOESN'T EVEN HAVE A DOORBELL.
KNOCK
KNOCK
KNOCK

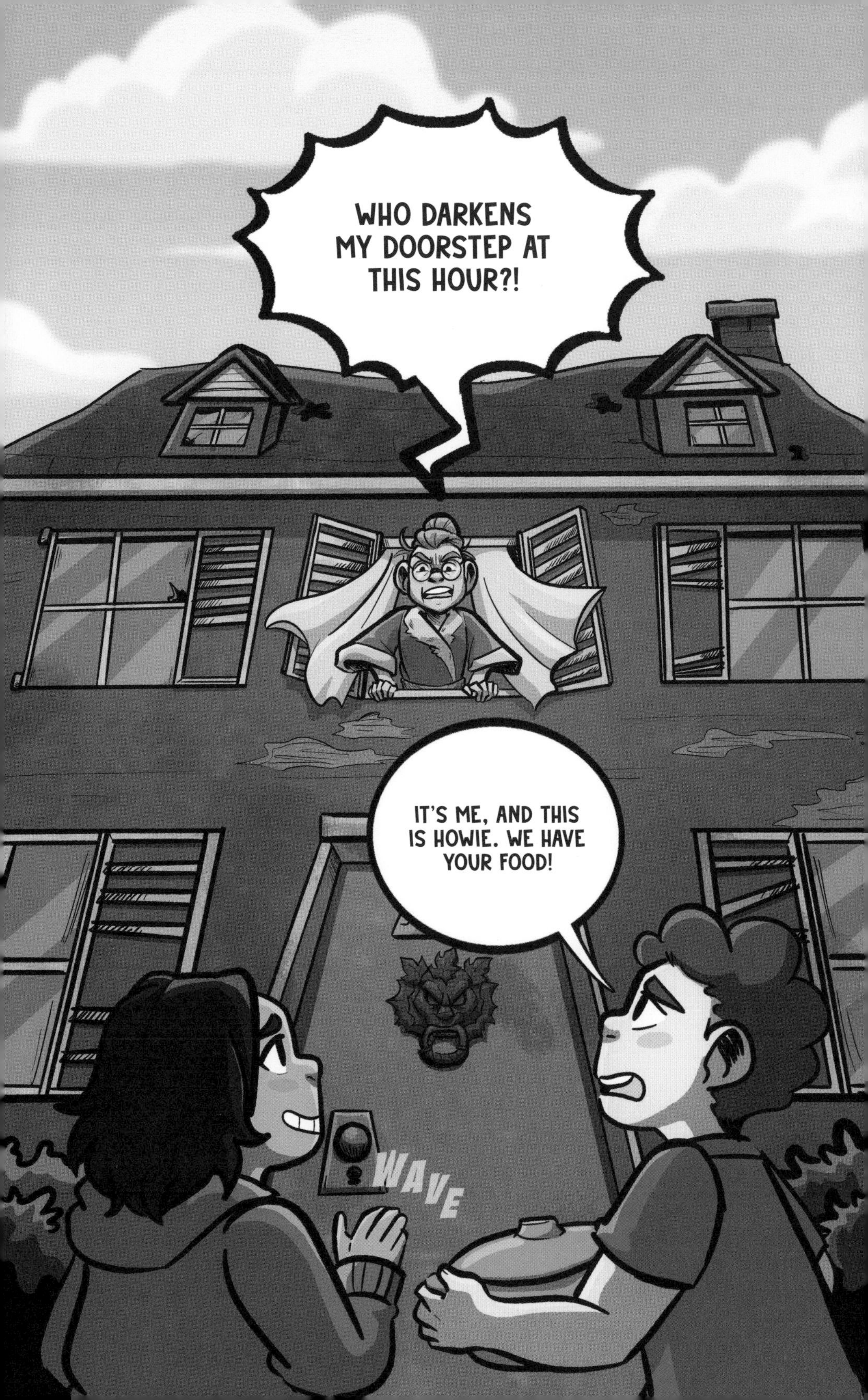
WHO DARKENS MY DOORSTEP AT THIS HOUR?!
IT'S ME, AND THIS IS HOWIE. WE HAVE YOUR FOOD!
WAVE

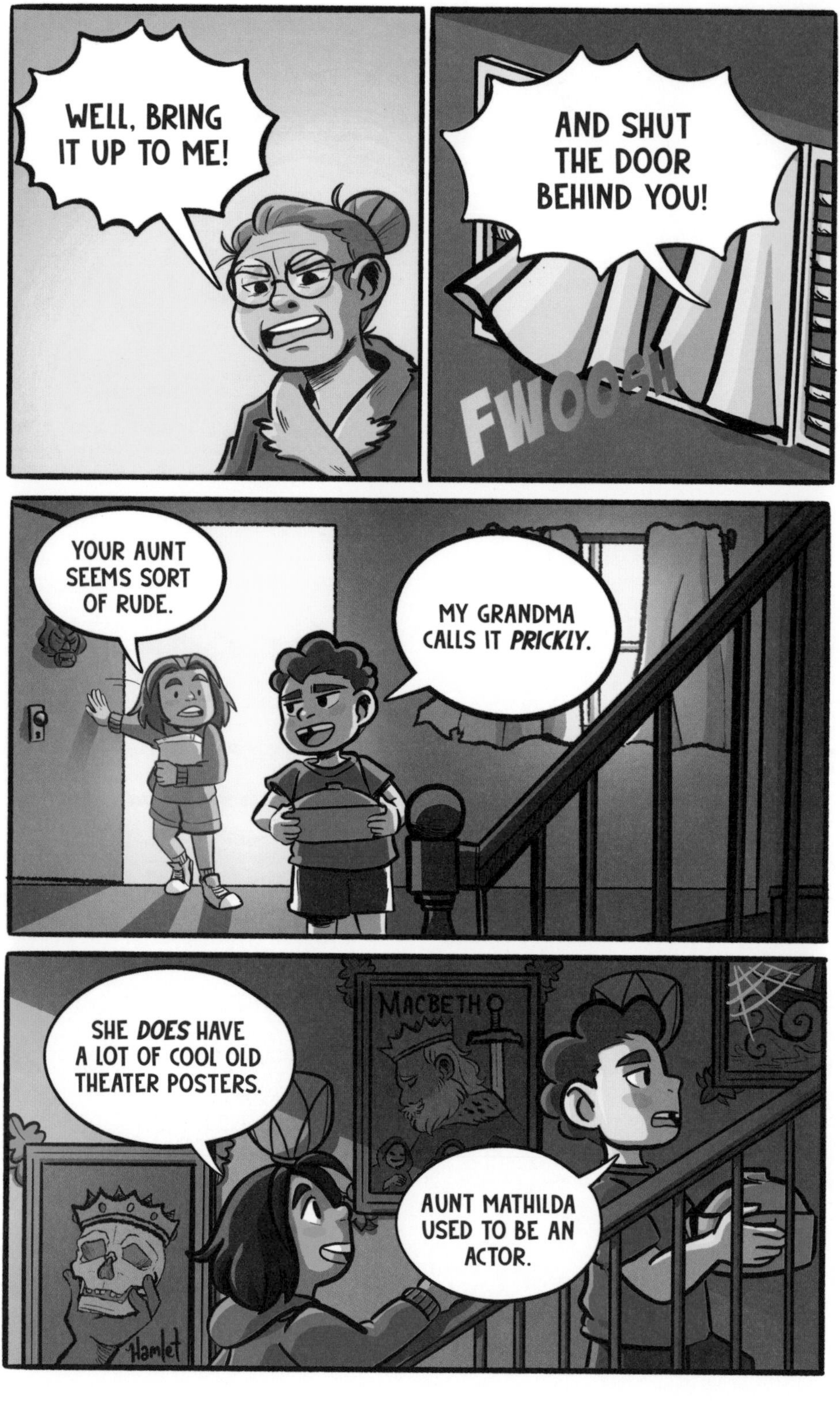
WELL, BRING IT UP TO ME!
AND SHUT THE DOOR BEHIND YOU!
FWOOSH
YOUR AUNT SEEMS SORT OF RUDE.
MY GRANDMA CALLS IT *PRICKLY*.
SHE *DOES* HAVE A LOT OF COOL OLD THEATER POSTERS.
MACBETH
Hamlet
AUNT MATHILDA USED TO BE AN ACTOR.

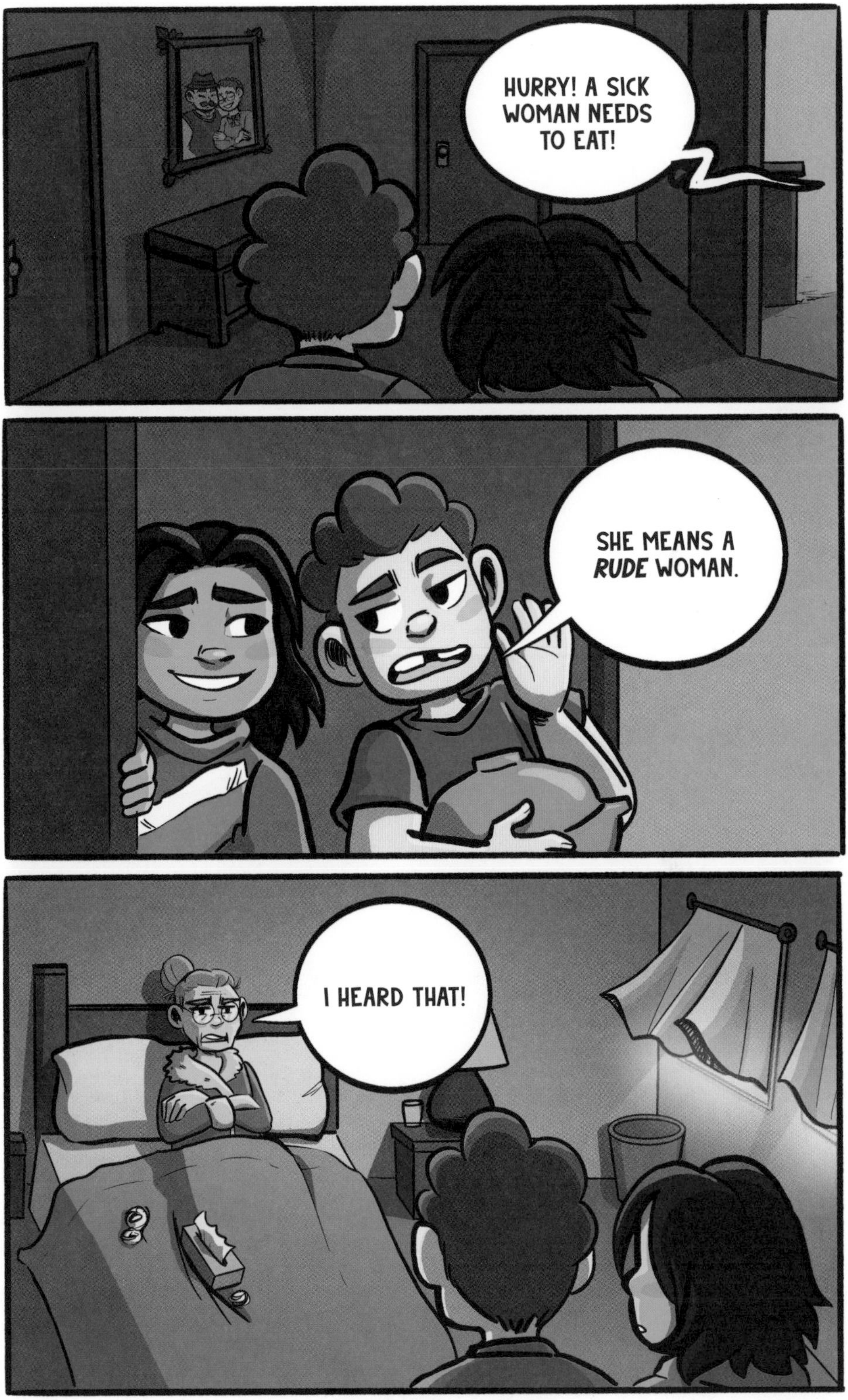
HURRY! A SICK WOMAN NEEDS TO EAT!
SHE MEANS A *RUDE* WOMAN.
I HEARD THAT!

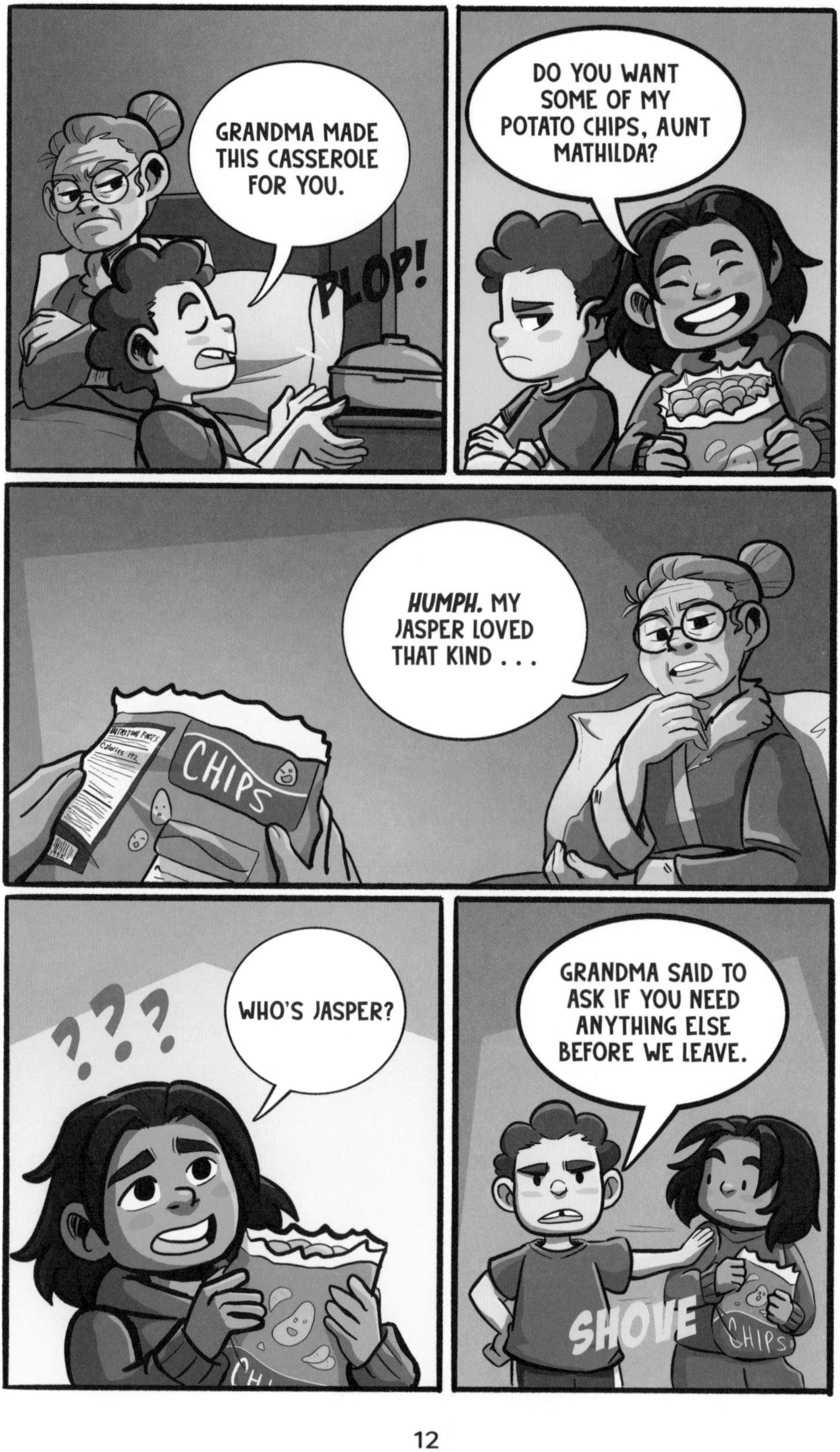
GRANDMA MADE THIS CASSEROLE FOR YOU.
PLOP!
DO YOU WANT SOME OF MY POTATO CHIPS, AUNT MATHILDA?
CHIPS
HUMPH. MY JASPER LOVED THAT KIND . . .
???
WHO'S JASPER?
GRANDMA SAID TO ASK IF YOU NEED ANYTHING ELSE BEFORE WE LEAVE.
SHOVE
CHIPS

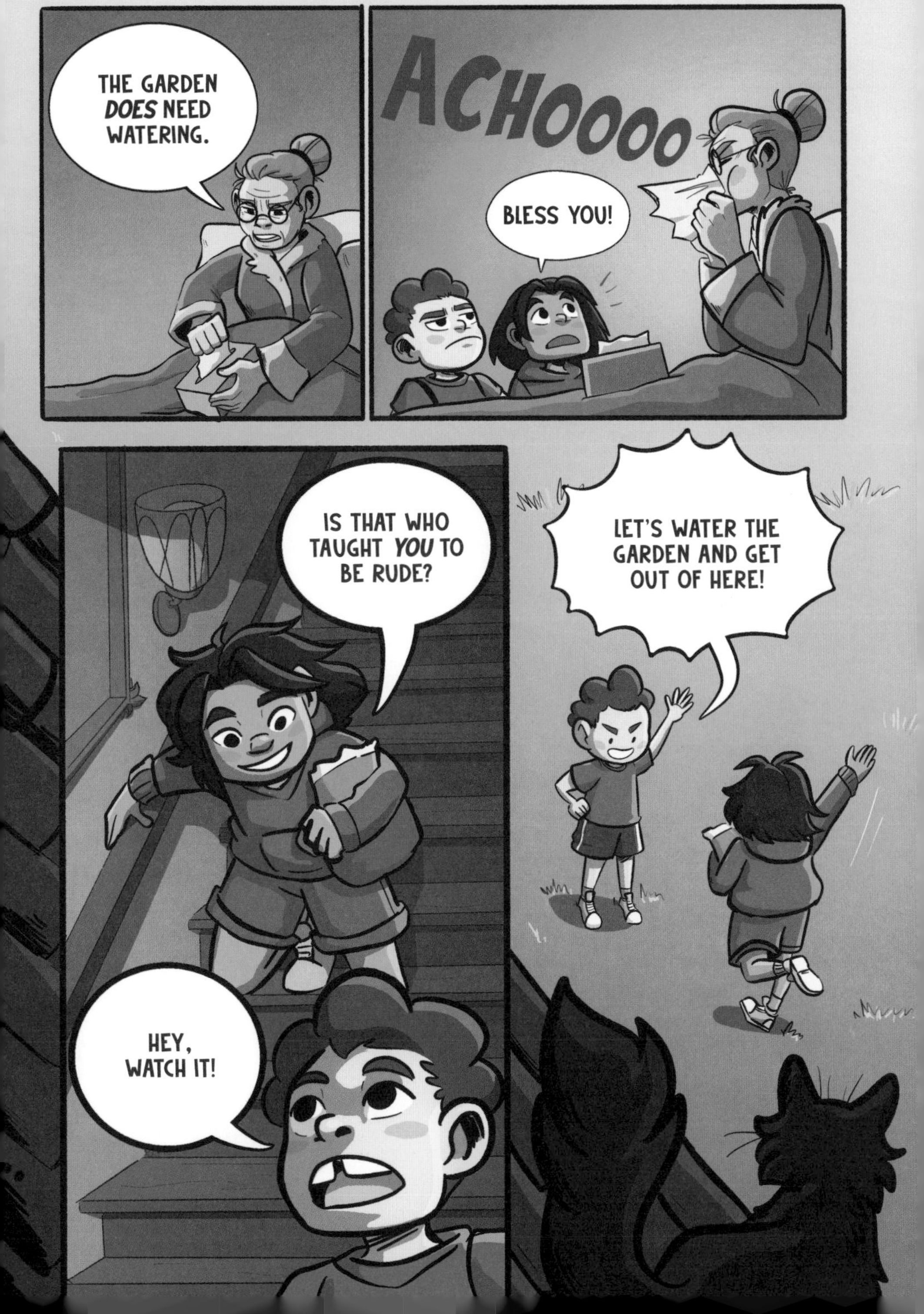
THE GARDEN *DOES* NEED WATERING.
ACHOOOO
BLESS YOU!
IS THAT WHO TAUGHT *YOU* TO BE RUDE?
HEY, WATCH IT!
LET'S WATER THE GARDEN AND GET OUT OF HERE!

CHAPTER 2 THE FACE IN THE WINDOW

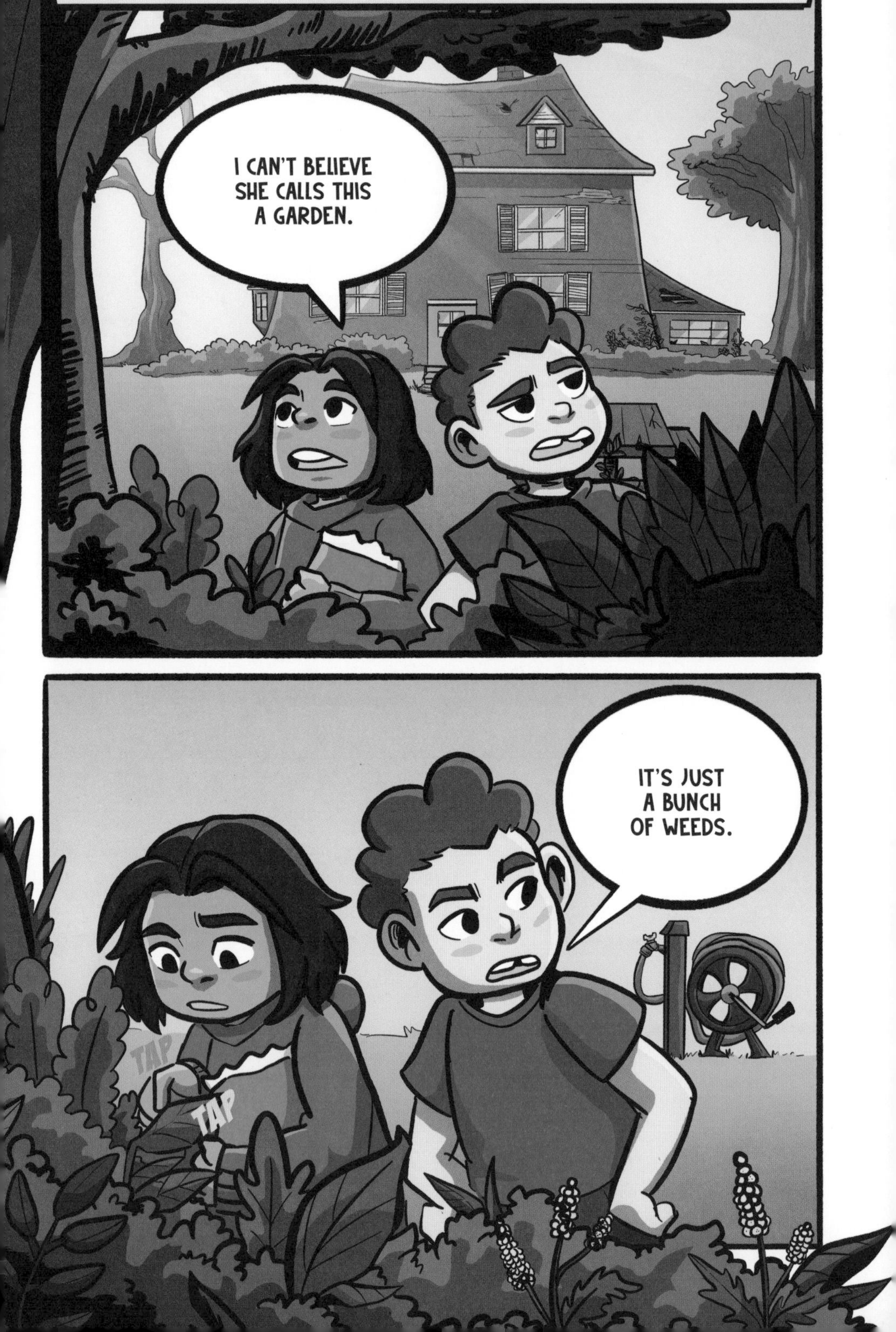
I CAN'T BELIEVE SHE CALLS THIS A GARDEN.
IT'S JUST A BUNCH OF WEEDS.
TAP
TAP

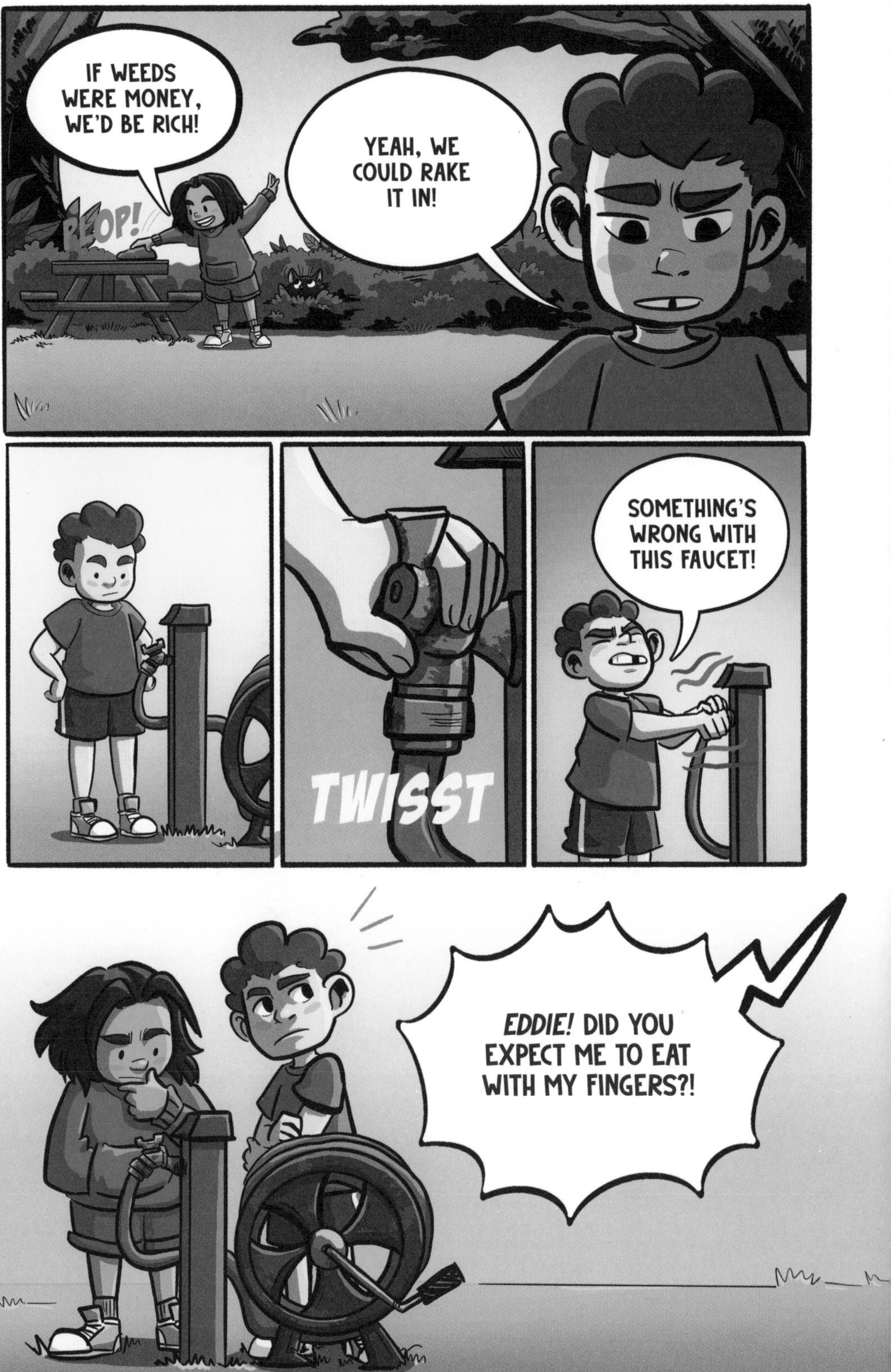
IF WEEDS WERE MONEY, WE'D BE RICH!
PLOP!
YEAH, WE COULD RAKE IT IN!
TWISST
SOMETHING'S WRONG WITH THIS FAUCET!
EDDIE! DID YOU EXPECT ME TO EAT WITH MY FINGERS?!

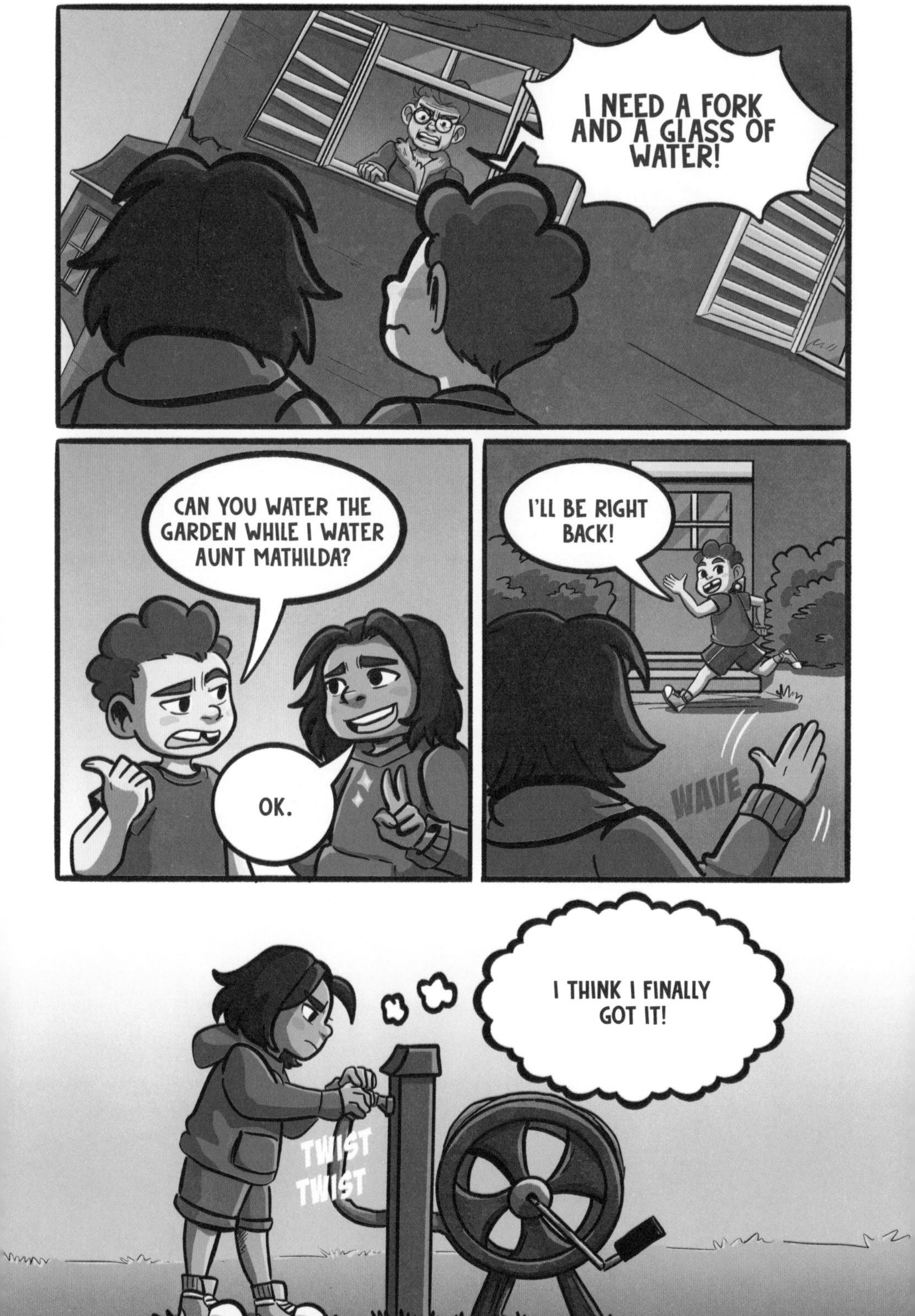

I NEED A FORK AND A GLASS OF WATER!
CAN YOU WATER THE GARDEN WHILE I WATER AUNT MATHILDA?
OK.
I'LL BE RIGHT BACK!
WAVE
I THINK I FINALLY GOT IT!
TWIST TWIST

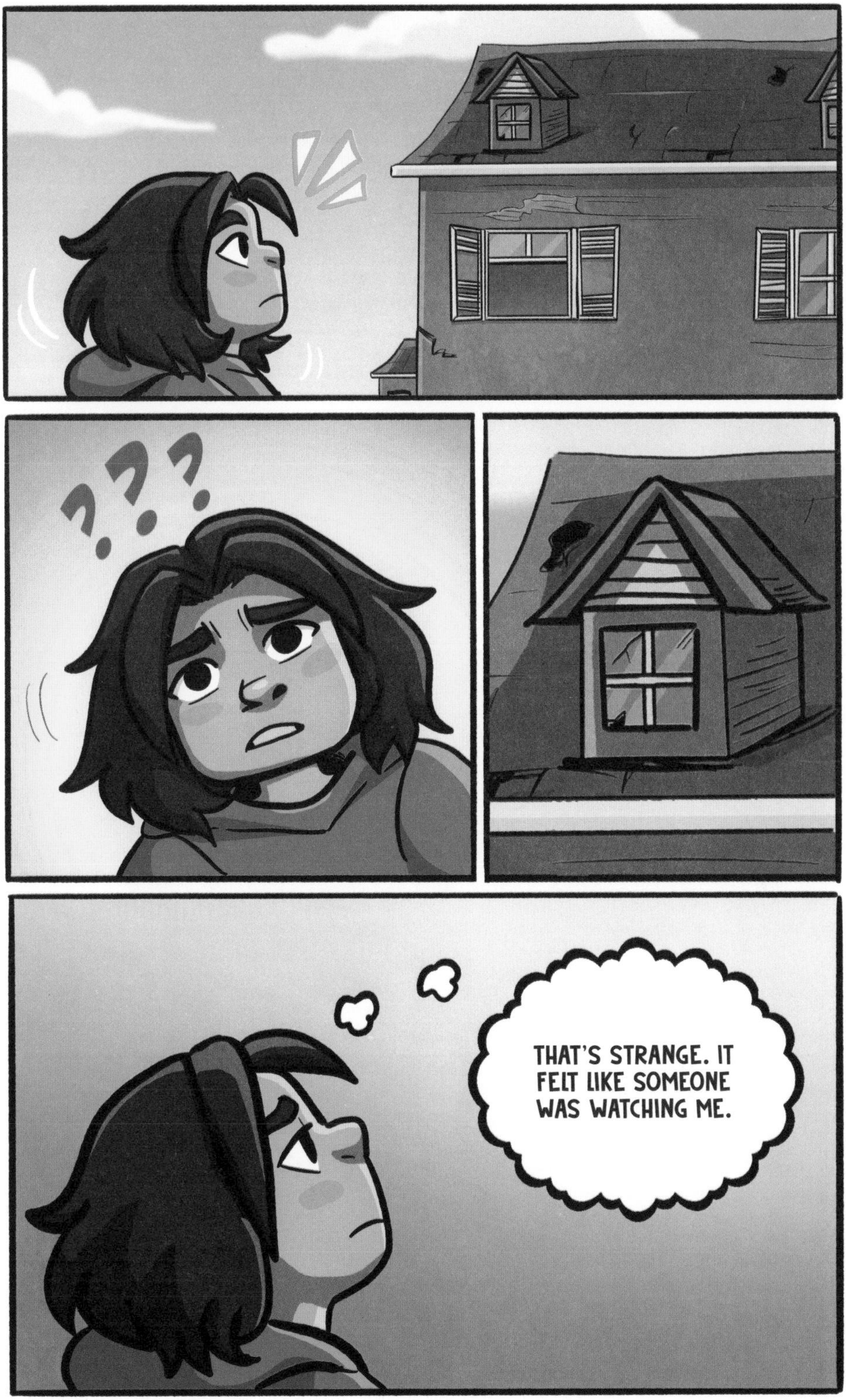
THAT'S STRANGE. IT
FELT LIKE SOMEONE
WAS WATCHING ME.

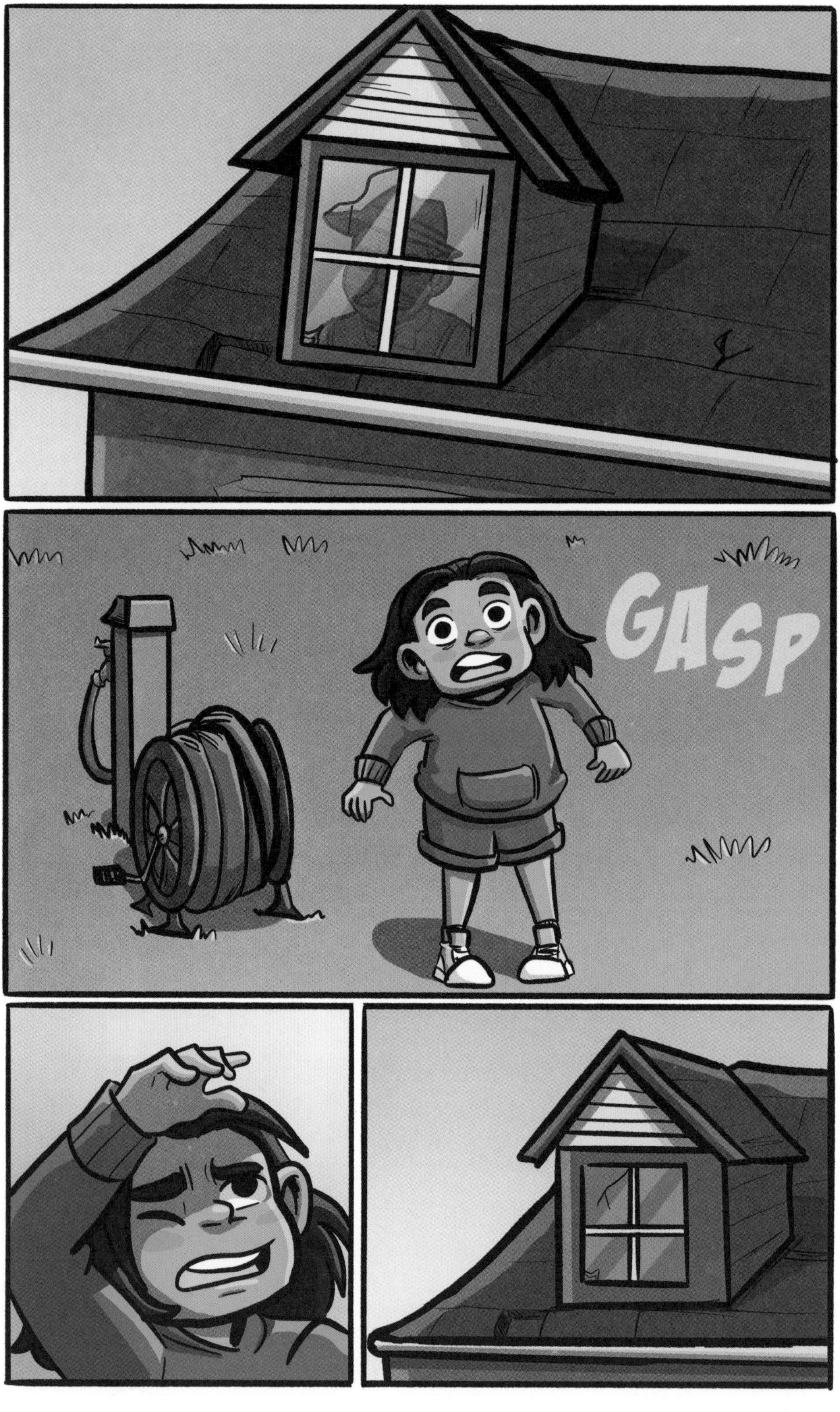
GASP

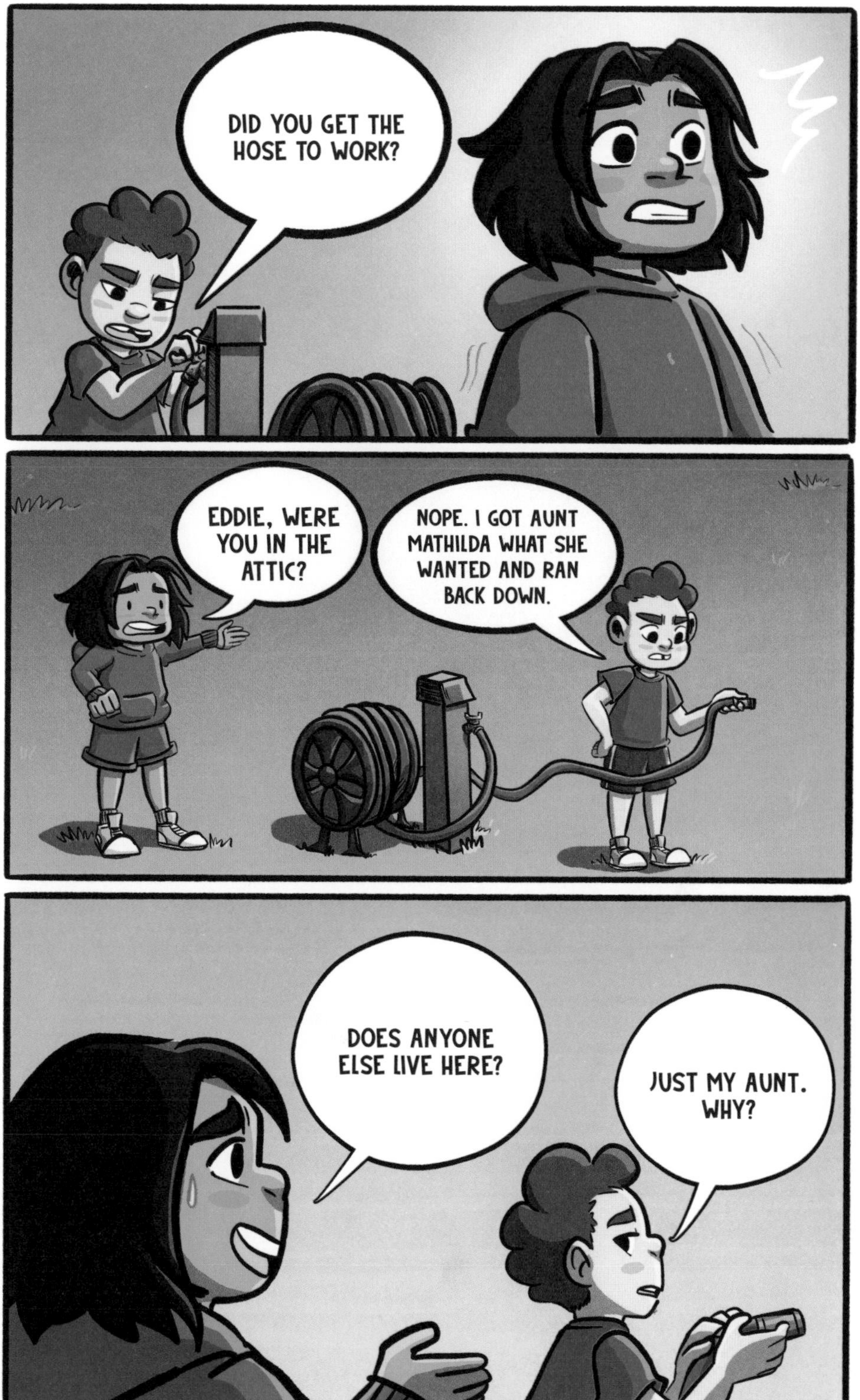
DID YOU GET THE HOSE TO WORK?
EDDIE, WERE YOU IN THE ATTIC?
NOPE. I GOT AUNT MATHILDA WHAT SHE WANTED AND RAN BACK DOWN.
DOES ANYONE ELSE LIVE HERE?
JUST MY AUNT. WHY?

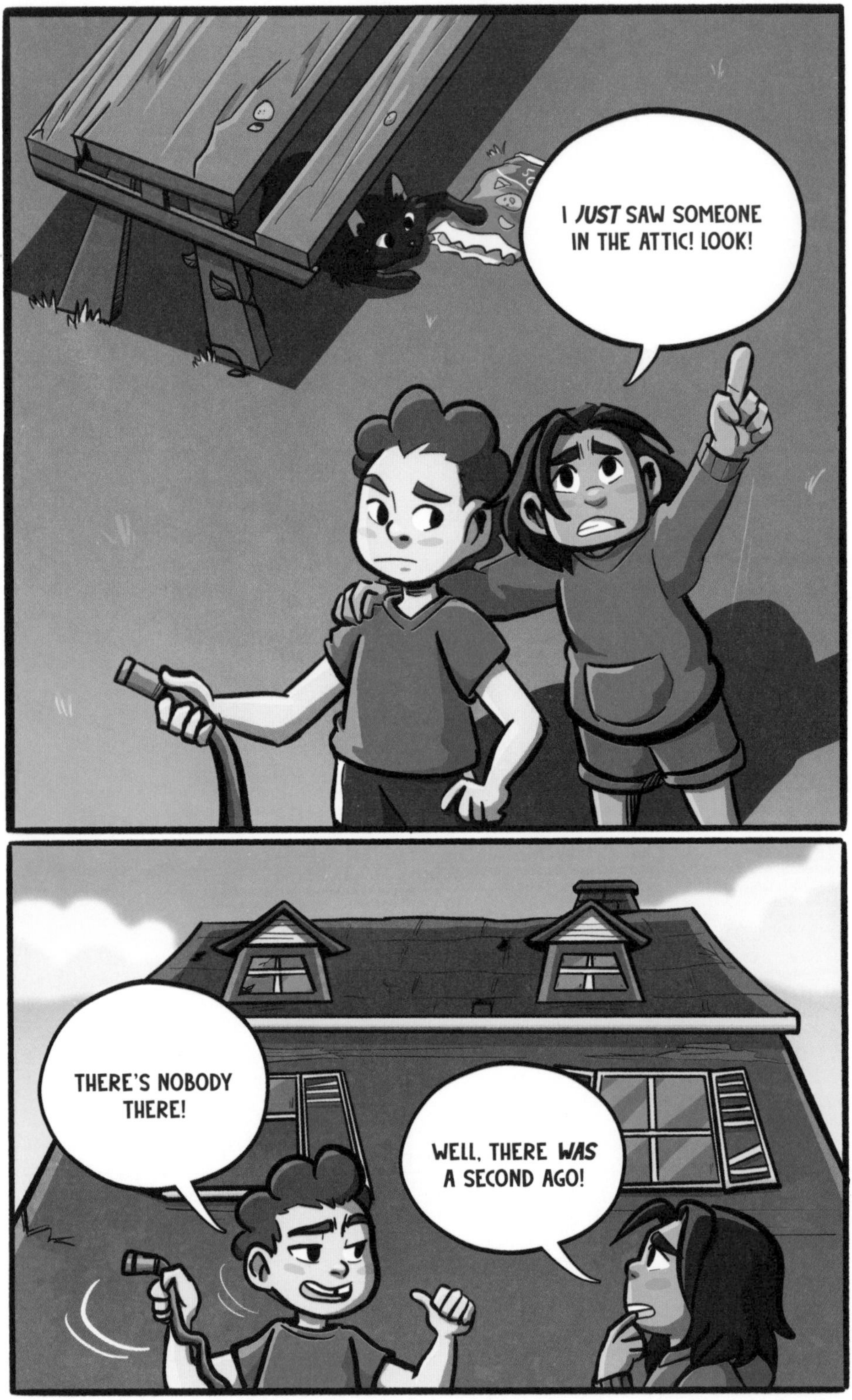
I *JUST* SAW SOMEONE IN THE ATTIC! LOOK!
THERE'S NOBODY THERE!
WELL, THERE *WAS* A SECOND AGO!

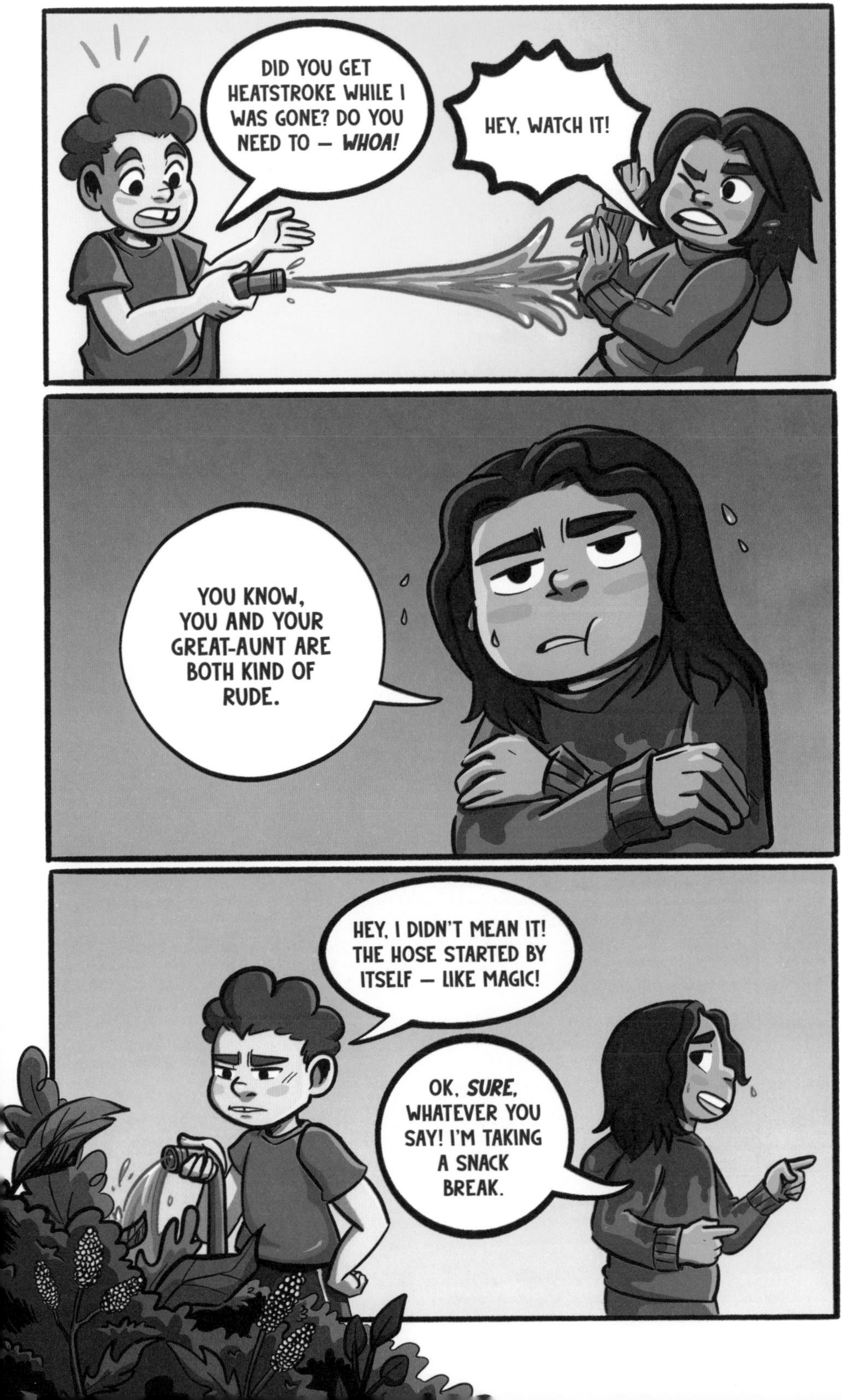
DID YOU GET HEATSTROKE WHILE I WAS GONE? DO YOU NEED TO — *WHOA!*
HEY, WATCH IT!
YOU KNOW, YOU AND YOUR GREAT-AUNT ARE BOTH KIND OF RUDE.
HEY, I DIDN'T MEAN IT! THE HOSE STARTED BY ITSELF — LIKE MAGIC!
OK, *SURE*, WHATEVER YOU SAY! I'M TAKING A SNACK BREAK.

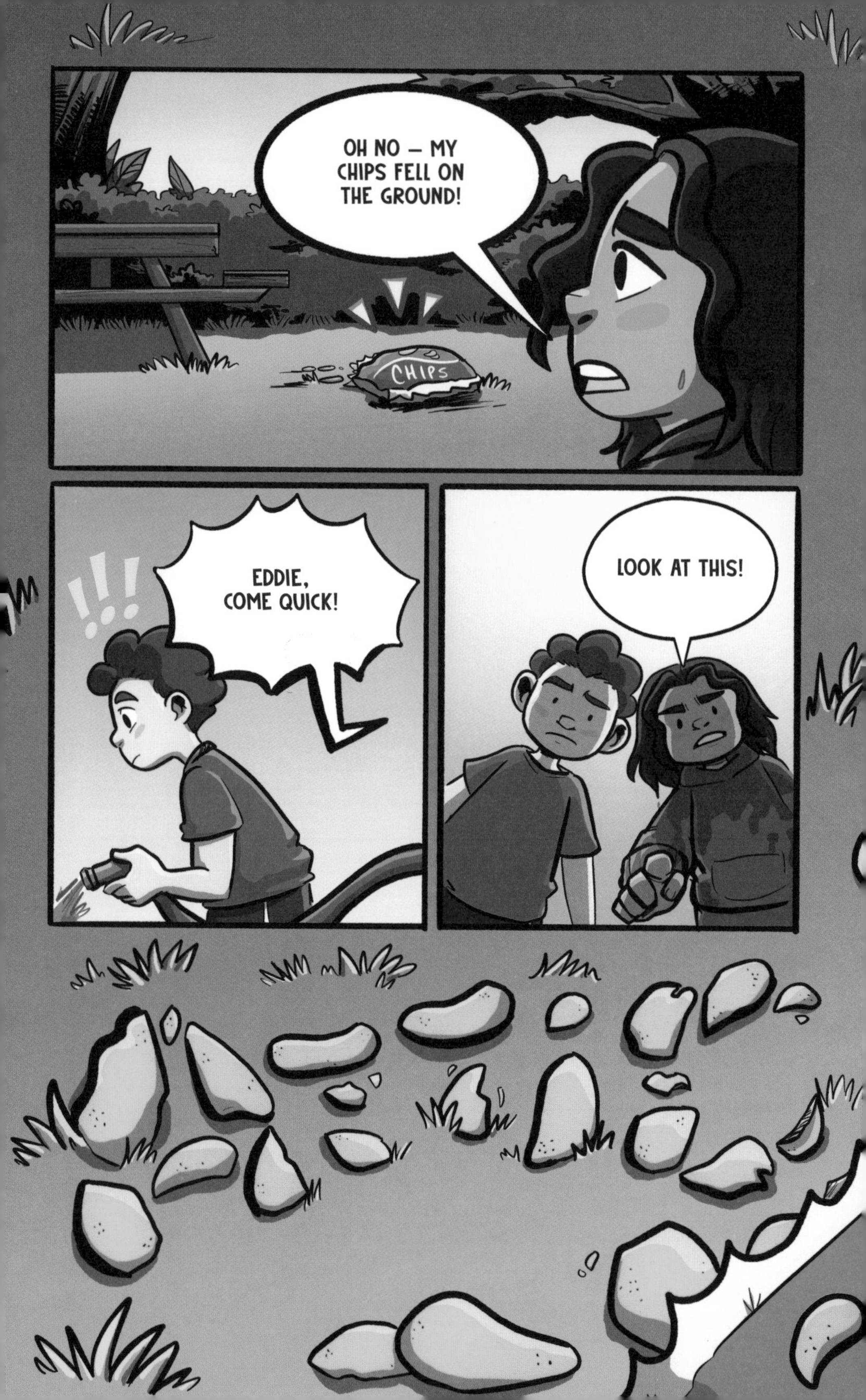
OH NO — MY CHIPS FELL ON THE GROUND!
CHIPS
EDDIE, COME QUICK!
LOOK AT THIS!

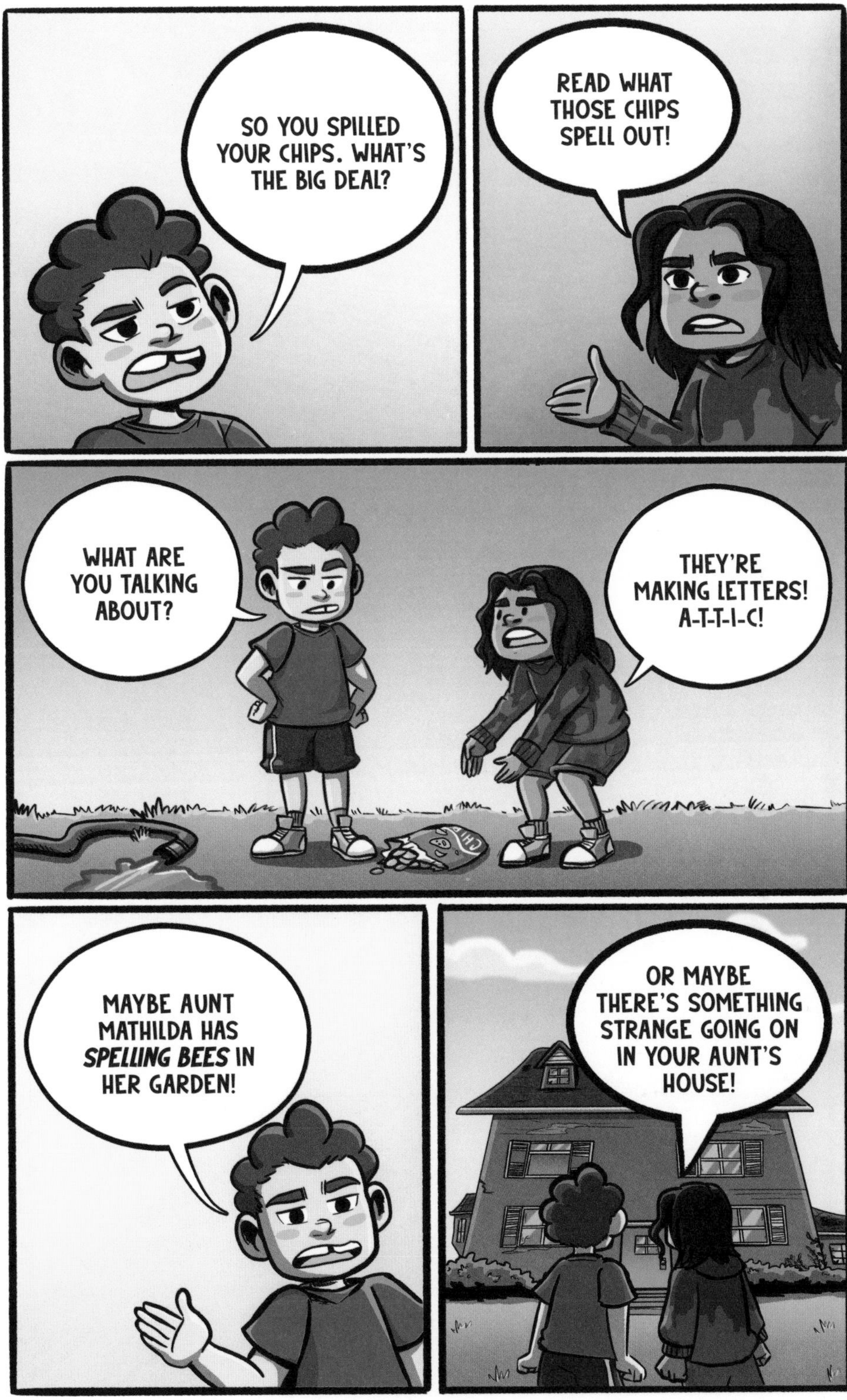
SO YOU SPILLED YOUR CHIPS. WHAT'S THE BIG DEAL?
READ WHAT THOSE CHIPS SPELL OUT!
WHAT ARE YOU TALKING ABOUT?
THEY'RE MAKING LETTERS! A-T-T-I-C!
CHIPS
MAYBE AUNT MATHILDA HAS *SPELLING BEES* IN HER GARDEN!
OR MAYBE THERE'S SOMETHING STRANGE GOING ON IN YOUR AUNT'S HOUSE!

CHAPTER 3 HAUNTED HOUSE

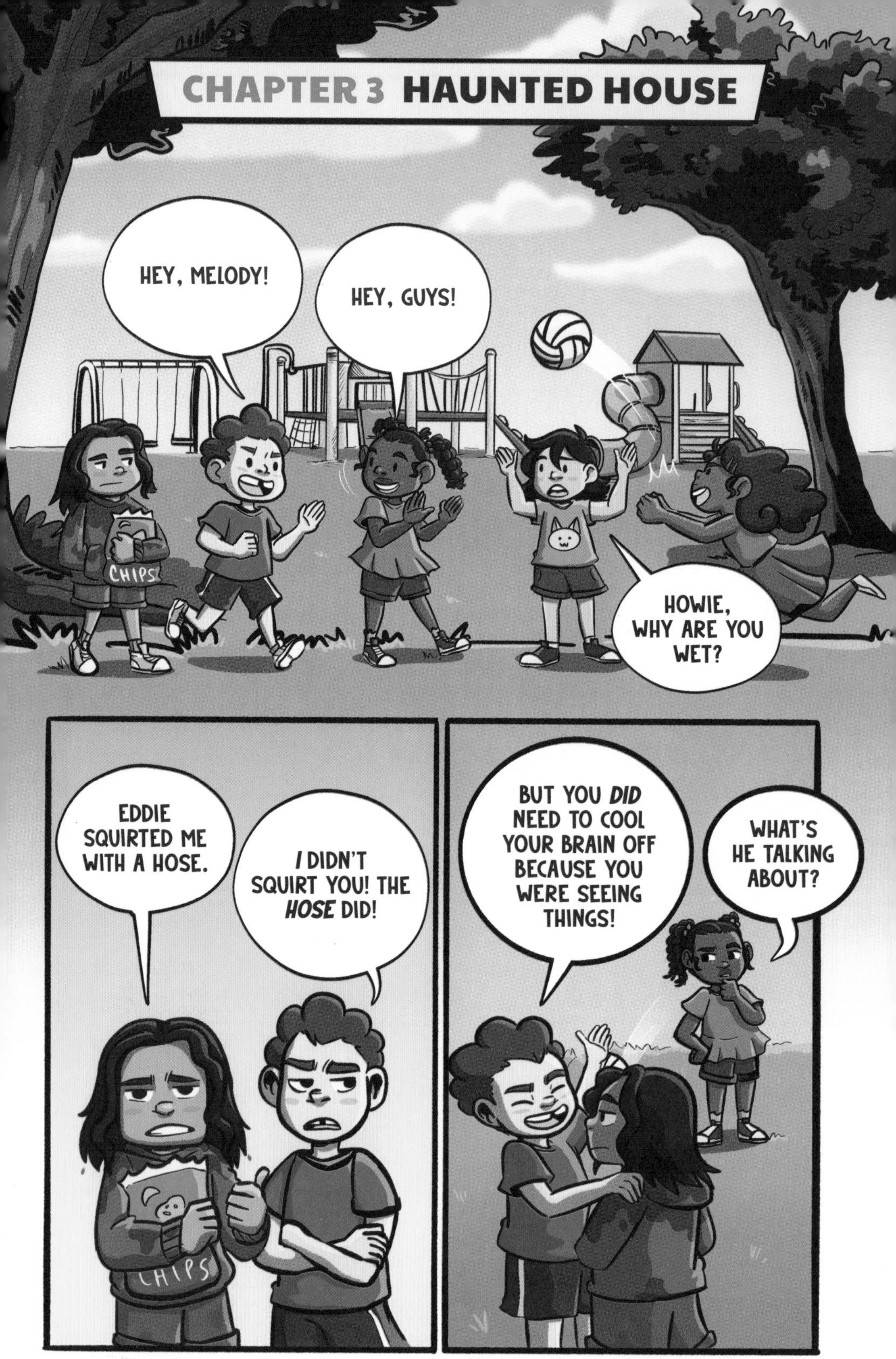
HEY, MELODY!
HEY, GUYS!
HOWIE, WHY ARE YOU WET?
CHIPS
EDDIE SQUIRTED ME WITH A HOSE.
I DIDN'T SQUIRT YOU! THE *HOSE* DID!
CHIPS
BUT YOU *DID* NEED TO COOL YOUR BRAIN OFF BECAUSE YOU WERE SEEING THINGS!
WHAT'S HE TALKING ABOUT?

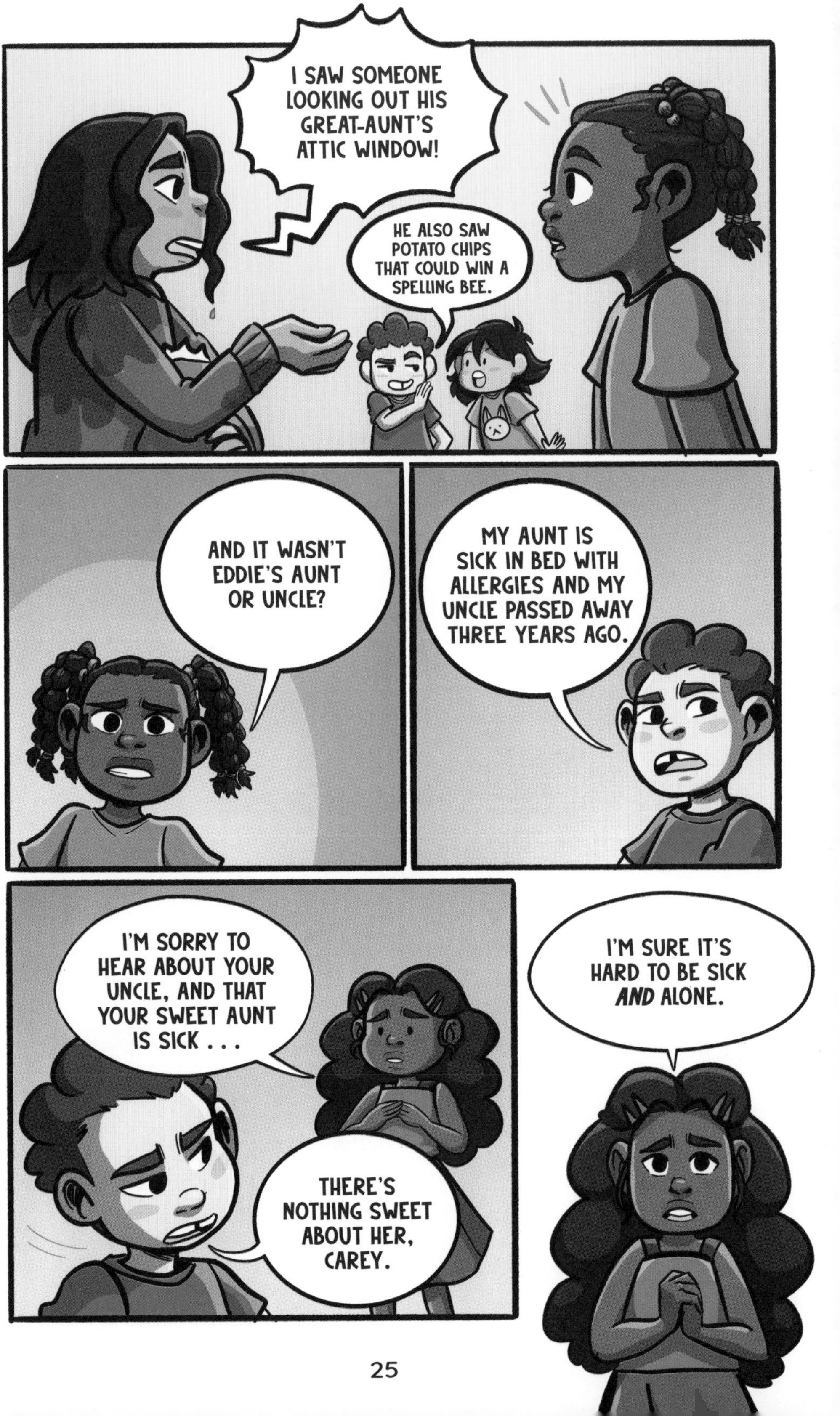
I SAW SOMEONE LOOKING OUT HIS GREAT-AUNT'S ATTIC WINDOW!
HE ALSO SAW POTATO CHIPS THAT COULD WIN A SPELLING BEE.
AND IT WASN'T EDDIE'S AUNT OR UNCLE?
MY AUNT IS SICK IN BED WITH ALLERGIES AND MY UNCLE PASSED AWAY THREE YEARS AGO.
I'M SORRY TO HEAR ABOUT YOUR UNCLE, AND THAT YOUR SWEET AUNT IS SICK . . .
THERE'S NOTHING SWEET ABOUT HER, CAREY.
I'M SURE IT'S HARD TO BE SICK *AND* ALONE.

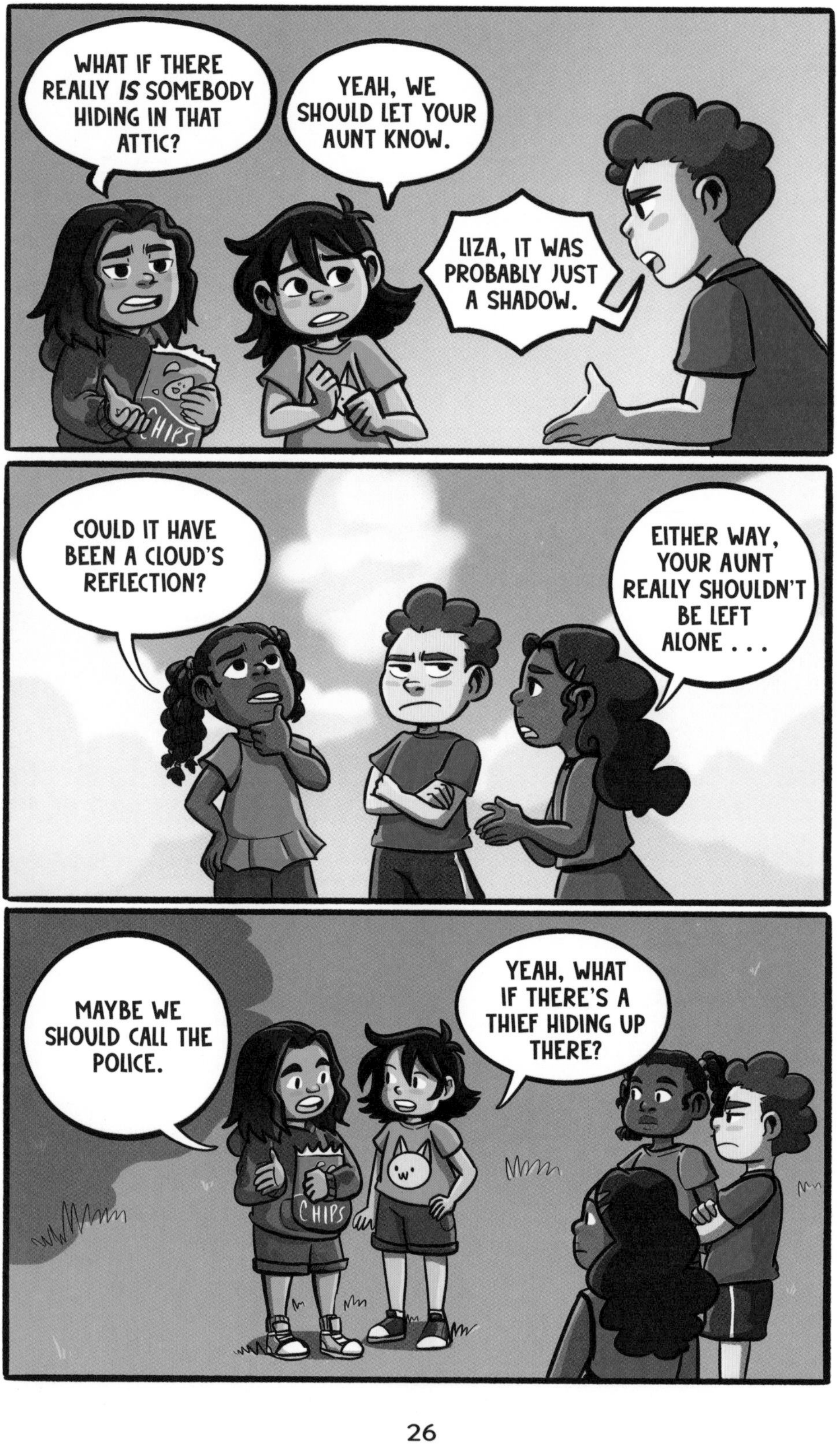
WHAT IF THERE REALLY *IS* SOMEBODY HIDING IN THAT ATTIC?
YEAH, WE SHOULD LET YOUR AUNT KNOW.
LIZA, IT WAS PROBABLY JUST A SHADOW.
COULD IT HAVE BEEN A CLOUD'S REFLECTION?
EITHER WAY, YOUR AUNT REALLY SHOULDN'T BE LEFT ALONE . . .
MAYBE WE SHOULD CALL THE POLICE.
YEAH, WHAT IF THERE'S A THIEF HIDING UP THERE?
CHIPS

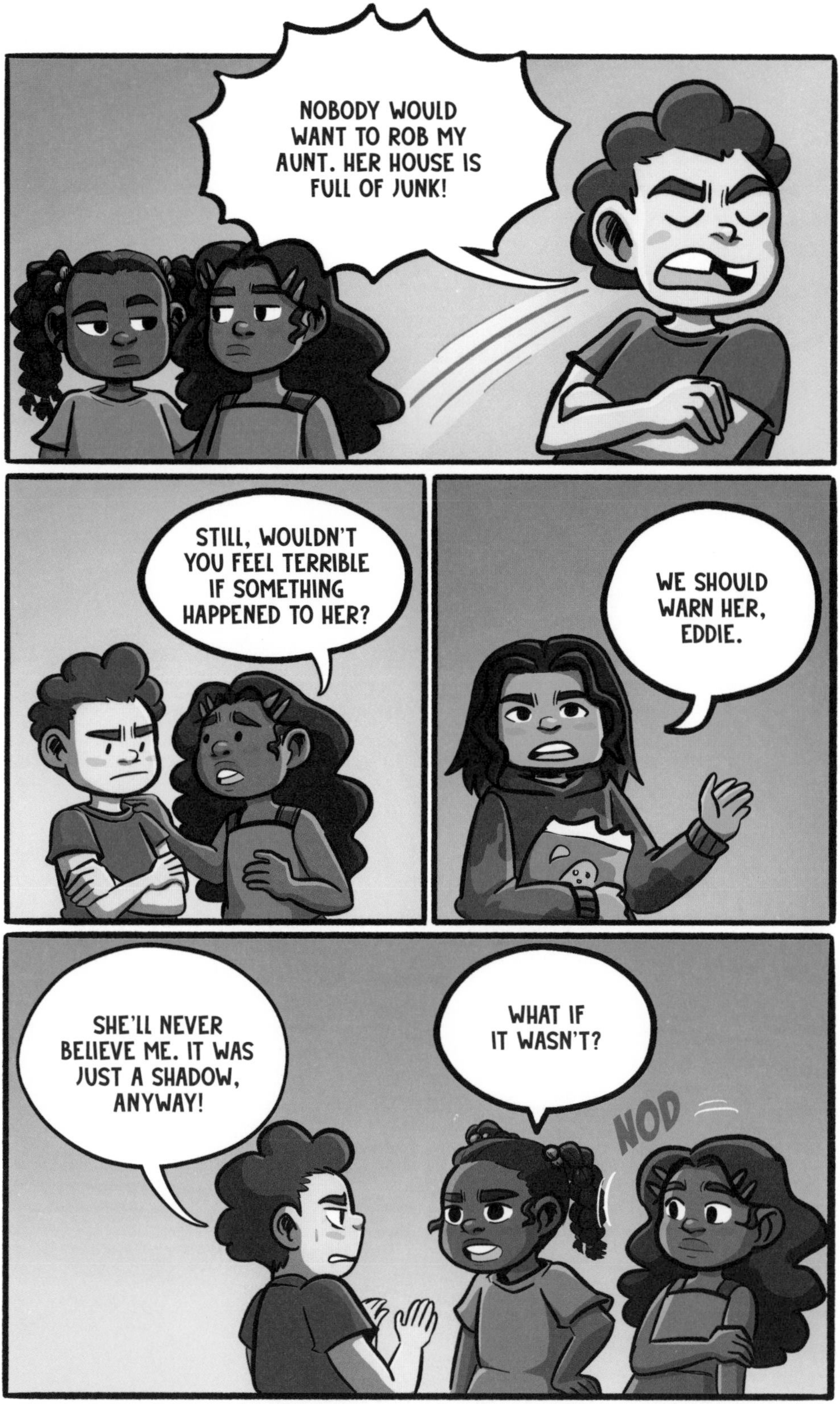
NOBODY WOULD WANT TO ROB MY AUNT. HER HOUSE IS FULL OF JUNK!
STILL, WOULDN'T YOU FEEL TERRIBLE IF SOMETHING HAPPENED TO HER?
WE SHOULD WARN HER, EDDIE.
SHE'LL NEVER BELIEVE ME. IT WAS JUST A SHADOW, ANYWAY!
WHAT IF IT WASN'T?
NOD

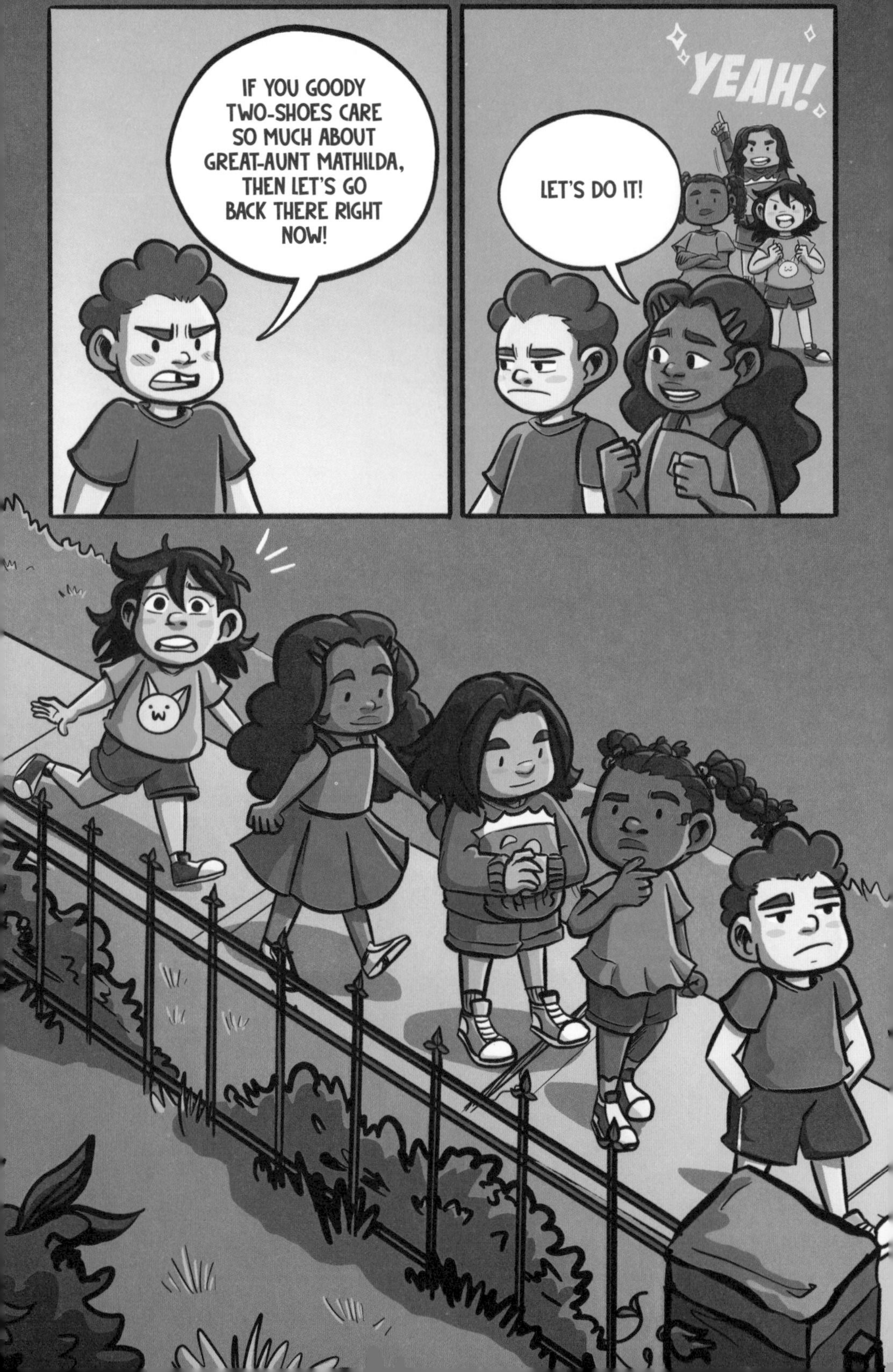
IF YOU GOODY TWO-SHOES CARE SO MUCH ABOUT GREAT-AUNT MATHILDA, THEN LET'S GO BACK THERE RIGHT NOW!
LET'S DO IT!
YEAH!

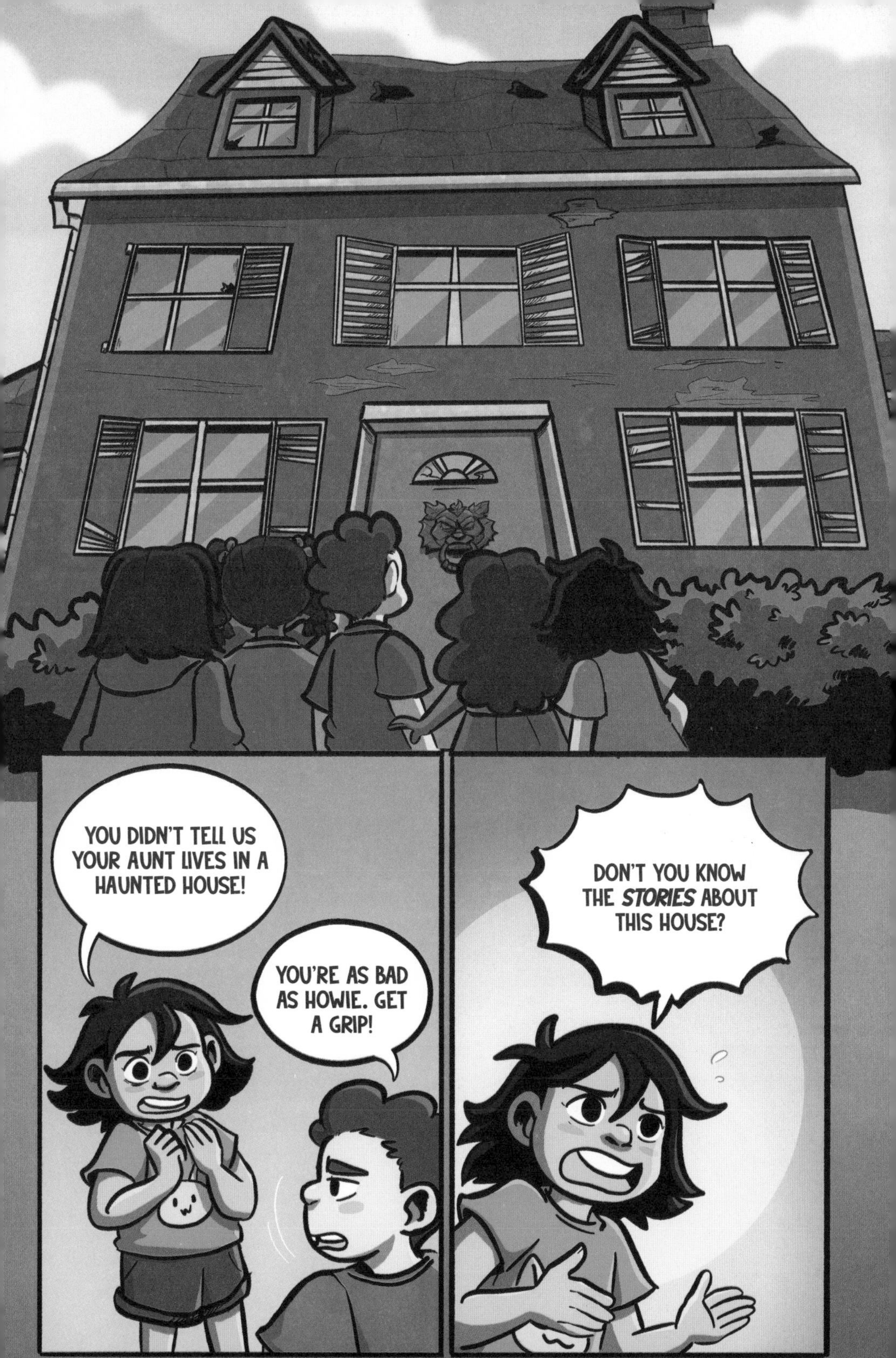
YOU DIDN'T TELL US YOUR AUNT LIVES IN A HAUNTED HOUSE!
YOU'RE AS BAD AS HOWIE. GET A GRIP!
DON'T YOU KNOW THE *STORIES* ABOUT THIS HOUSE?

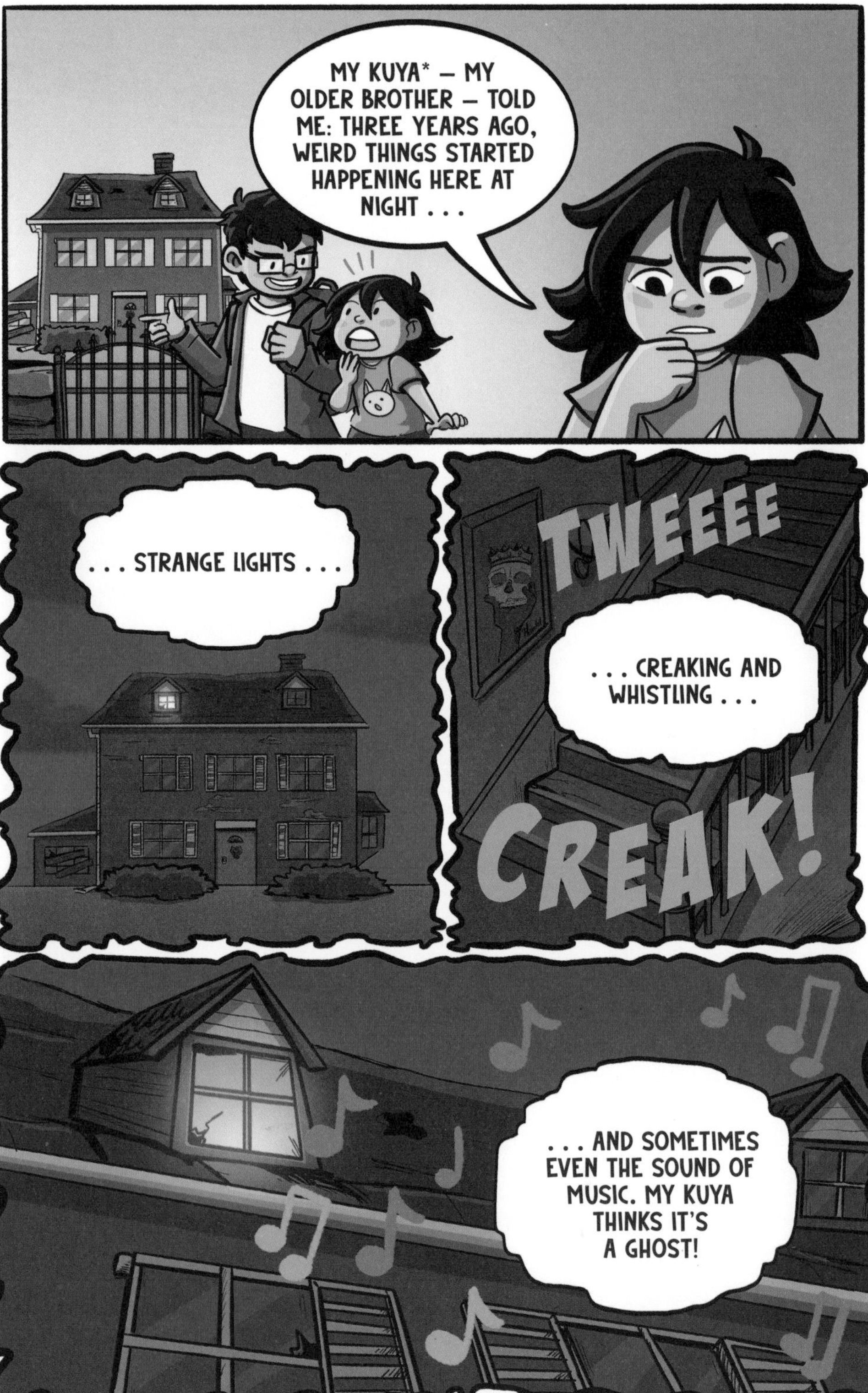
MY KUYA* – MY OLDER BROTHER – TOLD ME: THREE YEARS AGO, WEIRD THINGS STARTED HAPPENING HERE AT NIGHT . . .
. . . STRANGE LIGHTS . . .
TWEEEE
. . . CREAKING AND WHISTLING . . .
CREAK!
. . . AND SOMETIMES EVEN THE SOUND OF MUSIC. MY KUYA THINKS IT'S A GHOST!

*IN TAGALOG, A LANGUAGE OF THE PHILIPPINES, "KUYA" IS USED TO ADDRESS AN OLDER BROTHER OR RELATIVE AS A SIGN OF RESPECT.

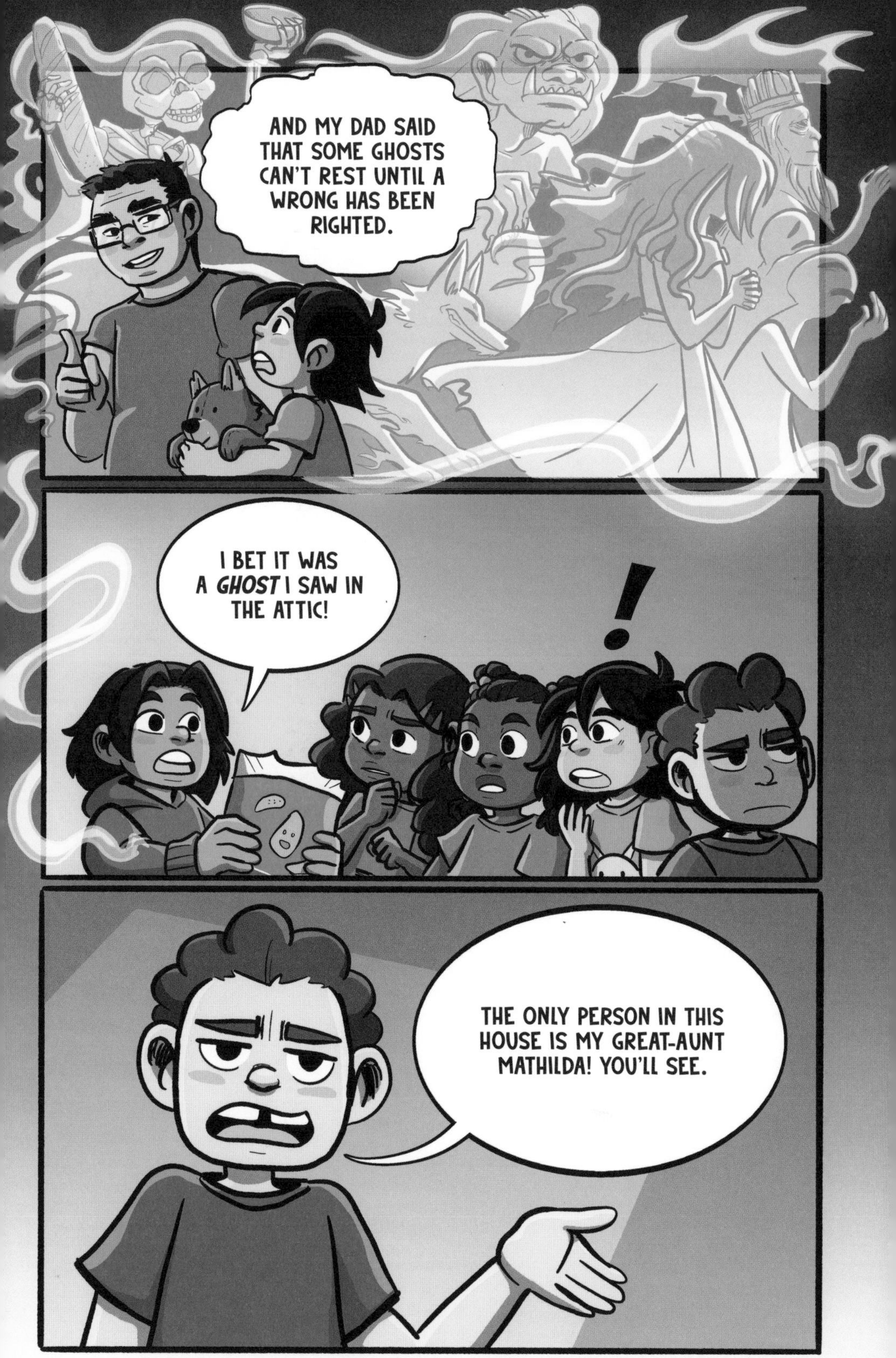
AND MY DAD SAID THAT SOME GHOSTS CAN'T REST UNTIL A WRONG HAS BEEN RIGHTED.
I BET IT WAS A *GHOST* I SAW IN THE ATTIC!
!
THE ONLY PERSON IN THIS HOUSE IS MY GREAT-AUNT MATHILDA! YOU'LL SEE.

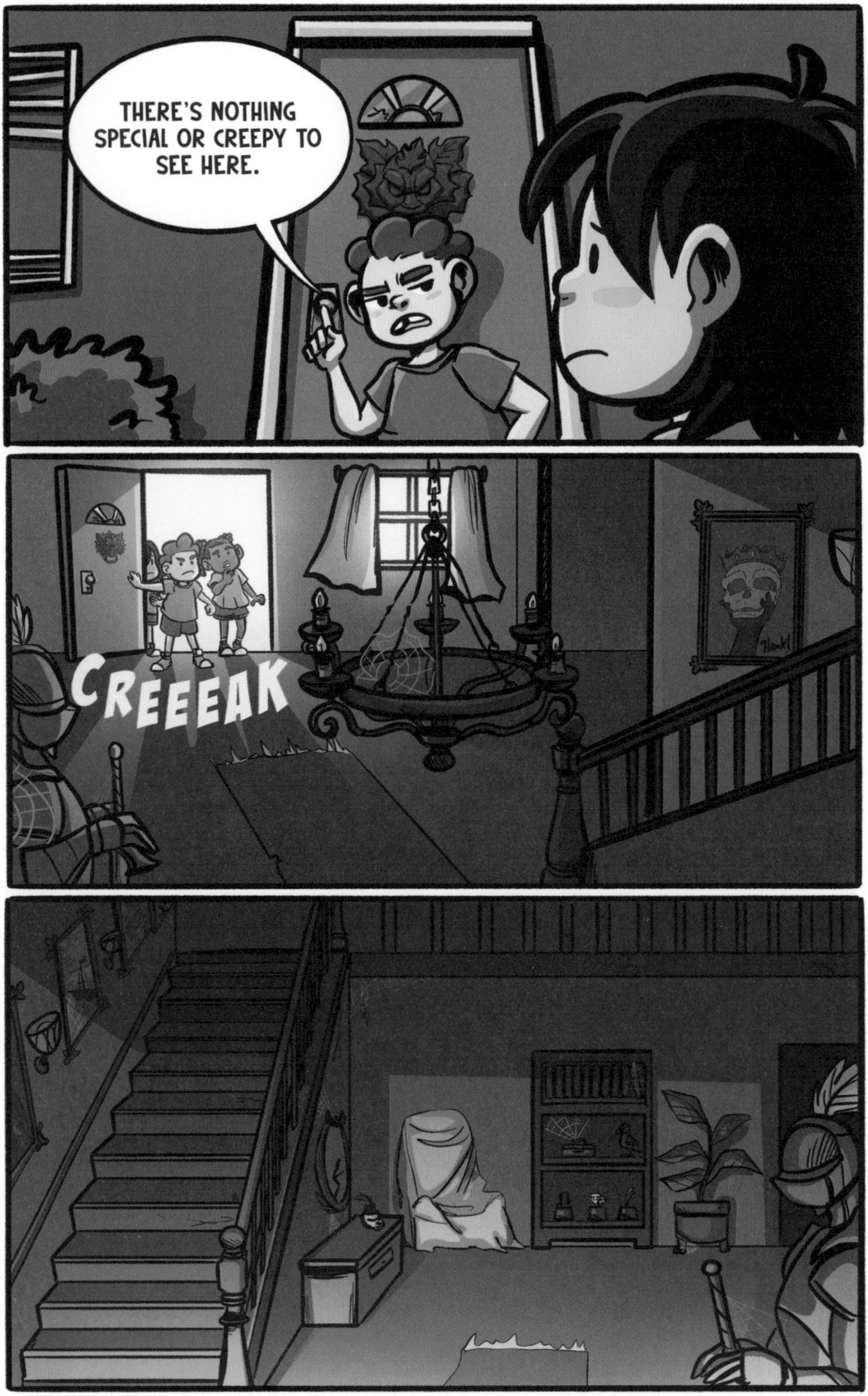
THERE'S NOTHING SPECIAL OR CREEPY TO SEE HERE.
CREEEAK

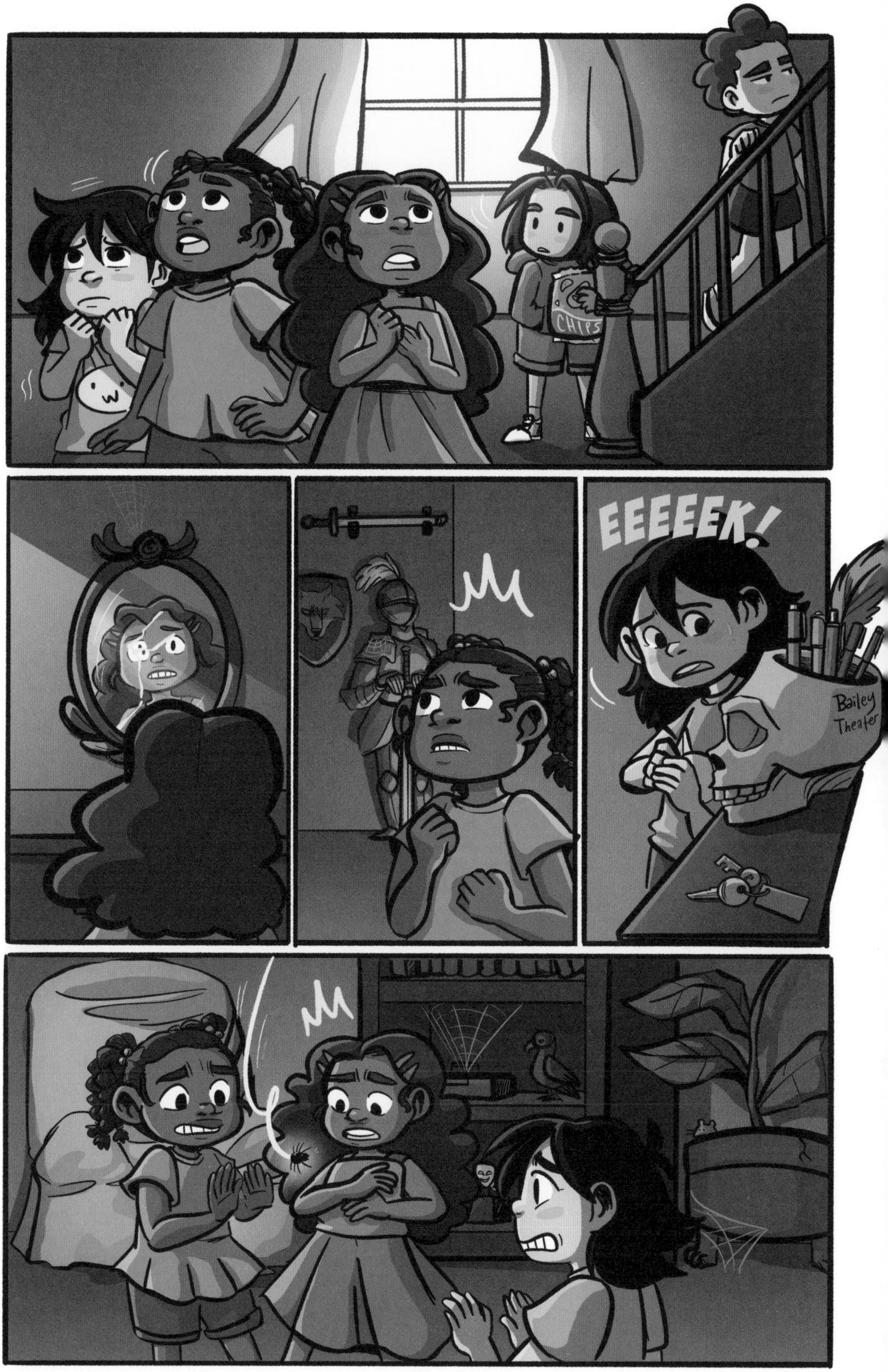
EEEEEK!
CHIPS
Bailey Theater

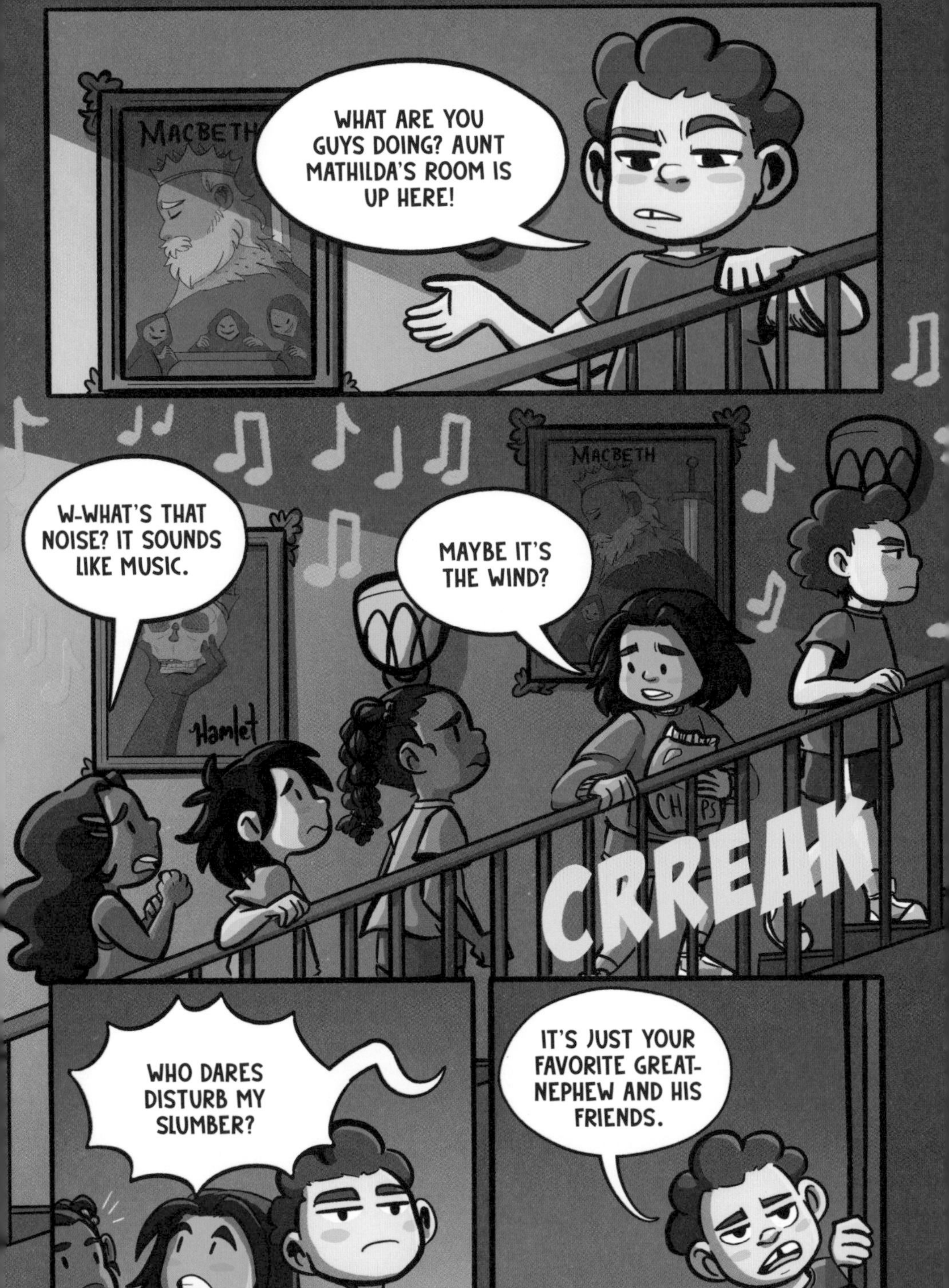
WHAT ARE YOU GUYS DOING? AUNT MATHILDA'S ROOM IS UP HERE!
MACBETH
W-WHAT'S THAT NOISE? IT SOUNDS LIKE MUSIC.
MAYBE IT'S THE WIND?
Hamlet
CHIPS
CRREAK
WHO DARES DISTURB MY SLUMBER?
IT'S JUST YOUR FAVORITE GREAT-NEPHEW AND HIS FRIENDS.

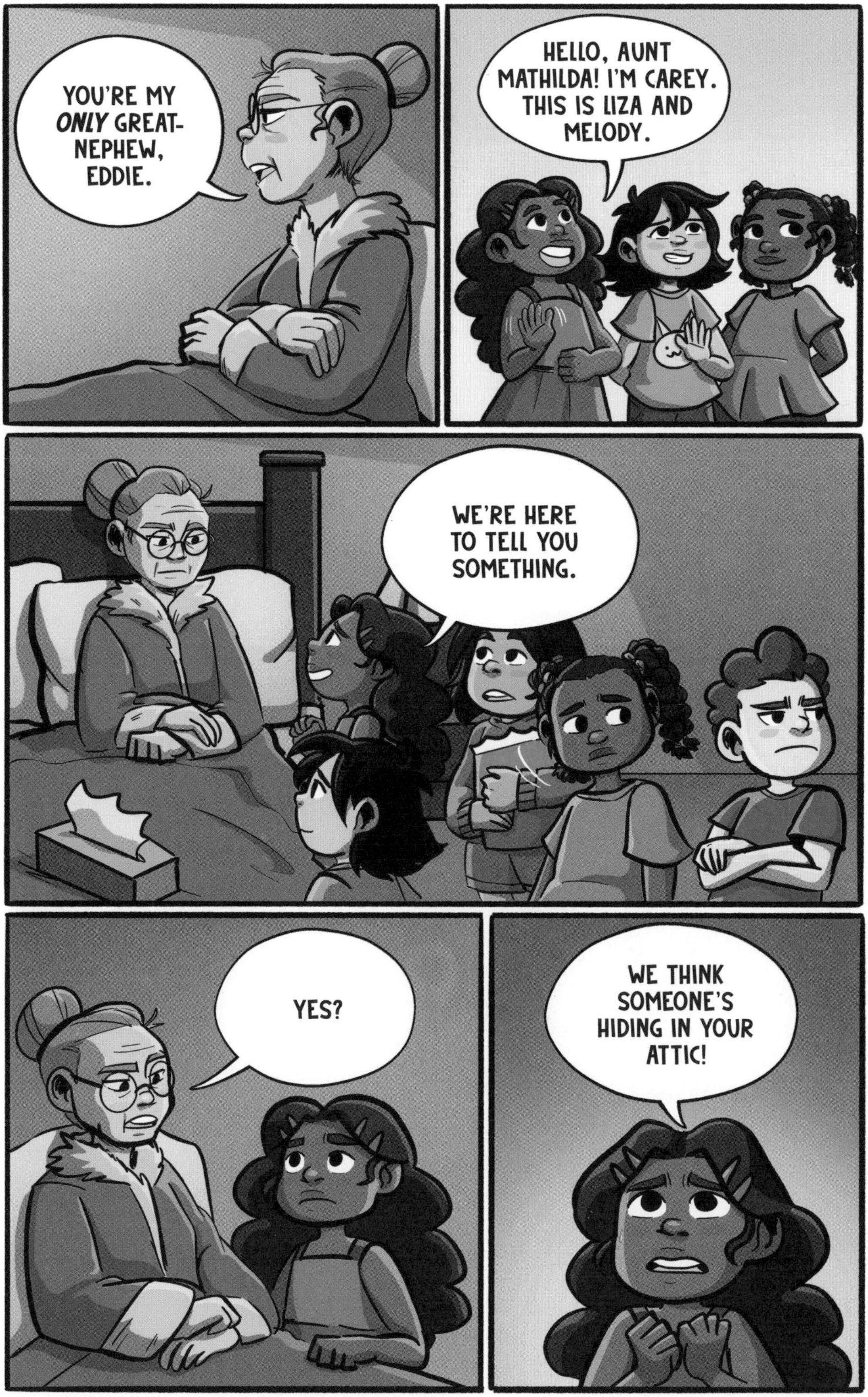
YOU'RE MY *ONLY* GREAT-NEPHEW, EDDIE.
HELLO, AUNT MATHILDA! I'M CAREY. THIS IS LIZA AND MELODY.
WE'RE HERE TO TELL YOU SOMETHING.
YES?
WE THINK SOMEONE'S HIDING IN YOUR ATTIC!

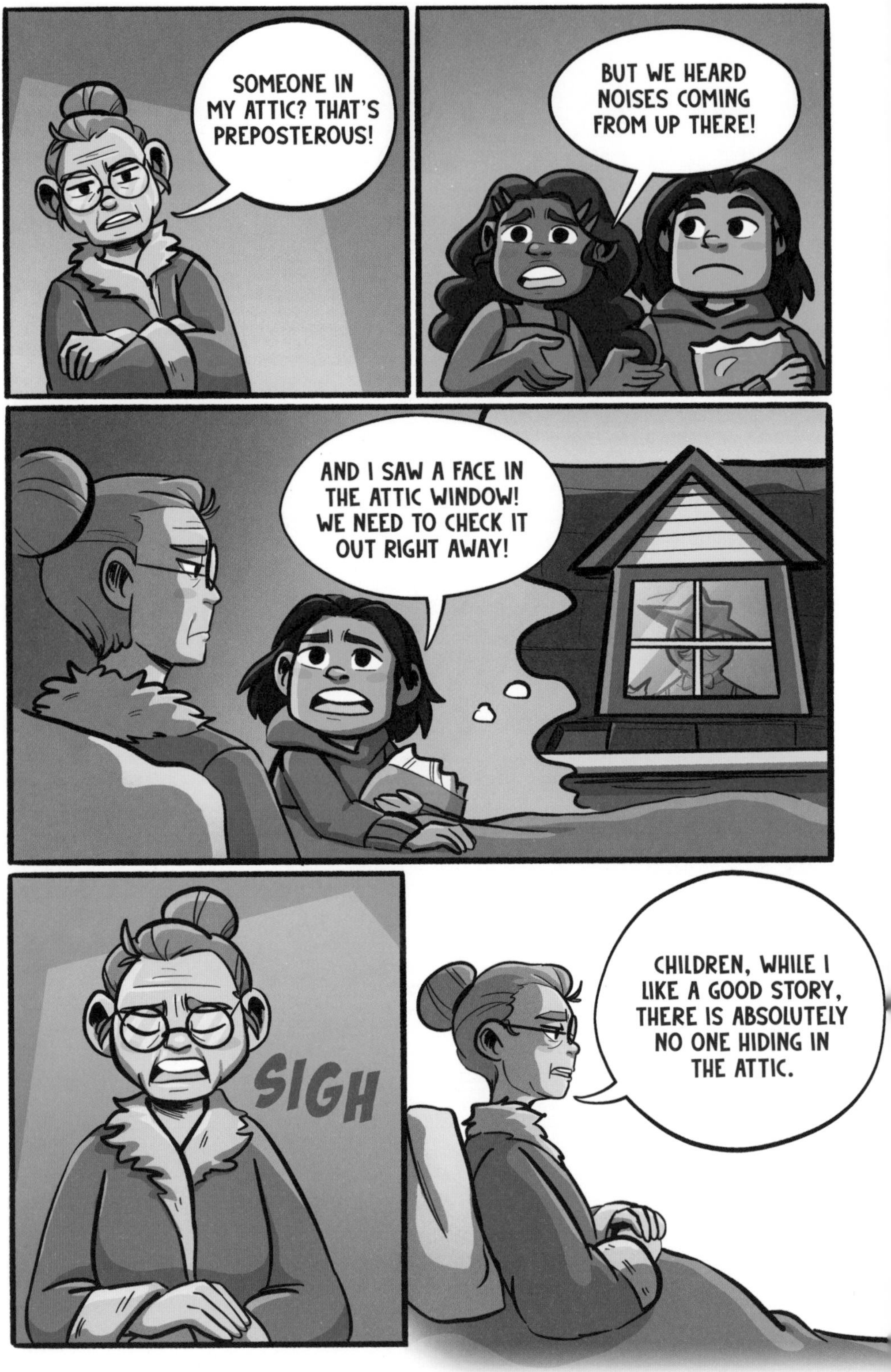
SOMEONE IN MY ATTIC? THAT'S PREPOSTEROUS!
BUT WE HEARD NOISES COMING FROM UP THERE!
AND I SAW A FACE IN THE ATTIC WINDOW! WE NEED TO CHECK IT OUT RIGHT AWAY!
SIGH
CHILDREN, WHILE I LIKE A GOOD STORY, THERE IS ABSOLUTELY NO ONE HIDING IN THE ATTIC.

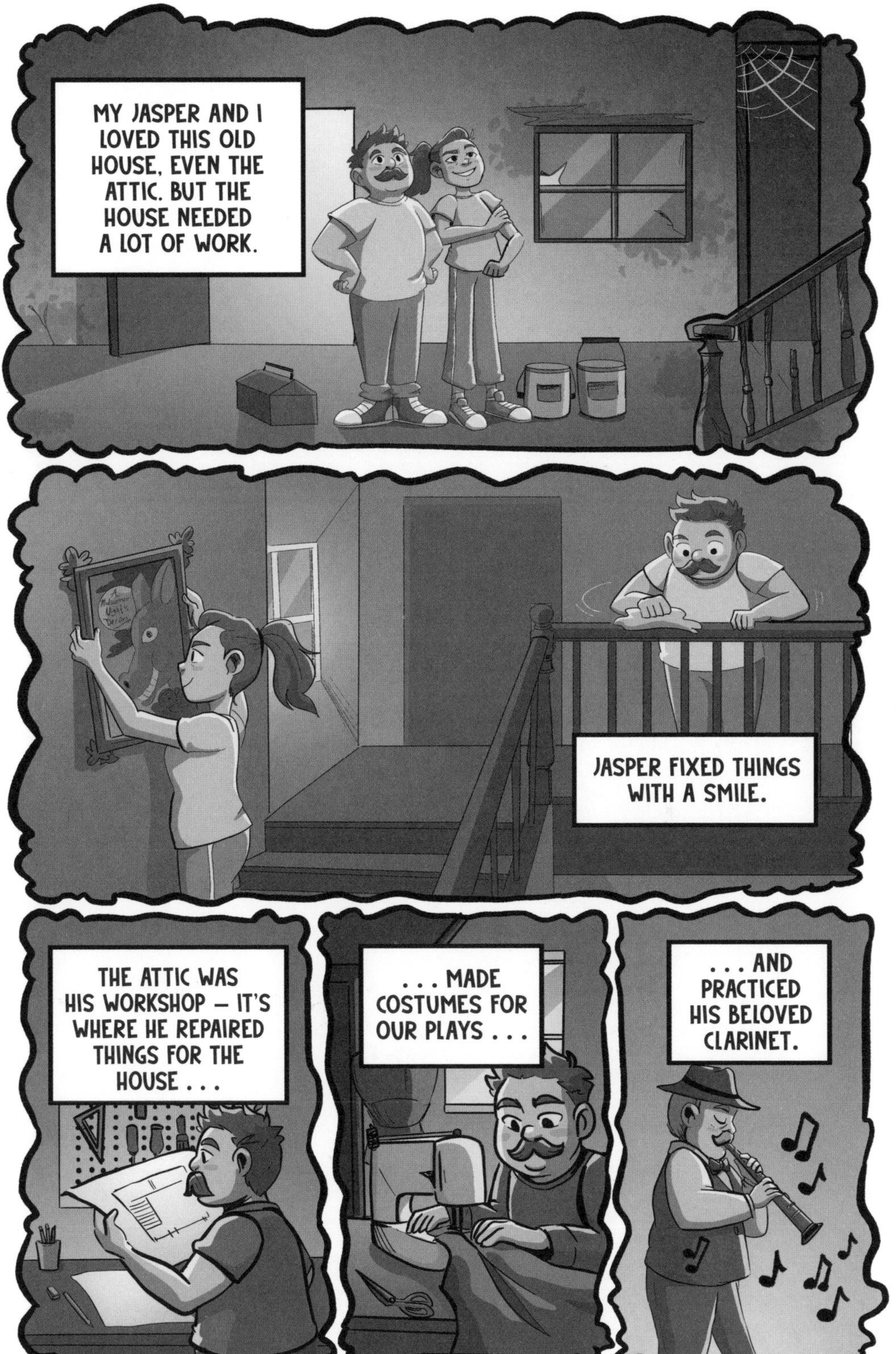
MY JASPER AND I LOVED THIS OLD HOUSE, EVEN THE ATTIC. BUT THE HOUSE NEEDED A LOT OF WORK.
JASPER FIXED THINGS WITH A SMILE.
THE ATTIC WAS HIS WORKSHOP — IT'S WHERE HE REPAIRED THINGS FOR THE HOUSE . . .
. . . MADE COSTUMES FOR OUR PLAYS . . .
. . . AND PRACTICED HIS BELOVED CLARINET.

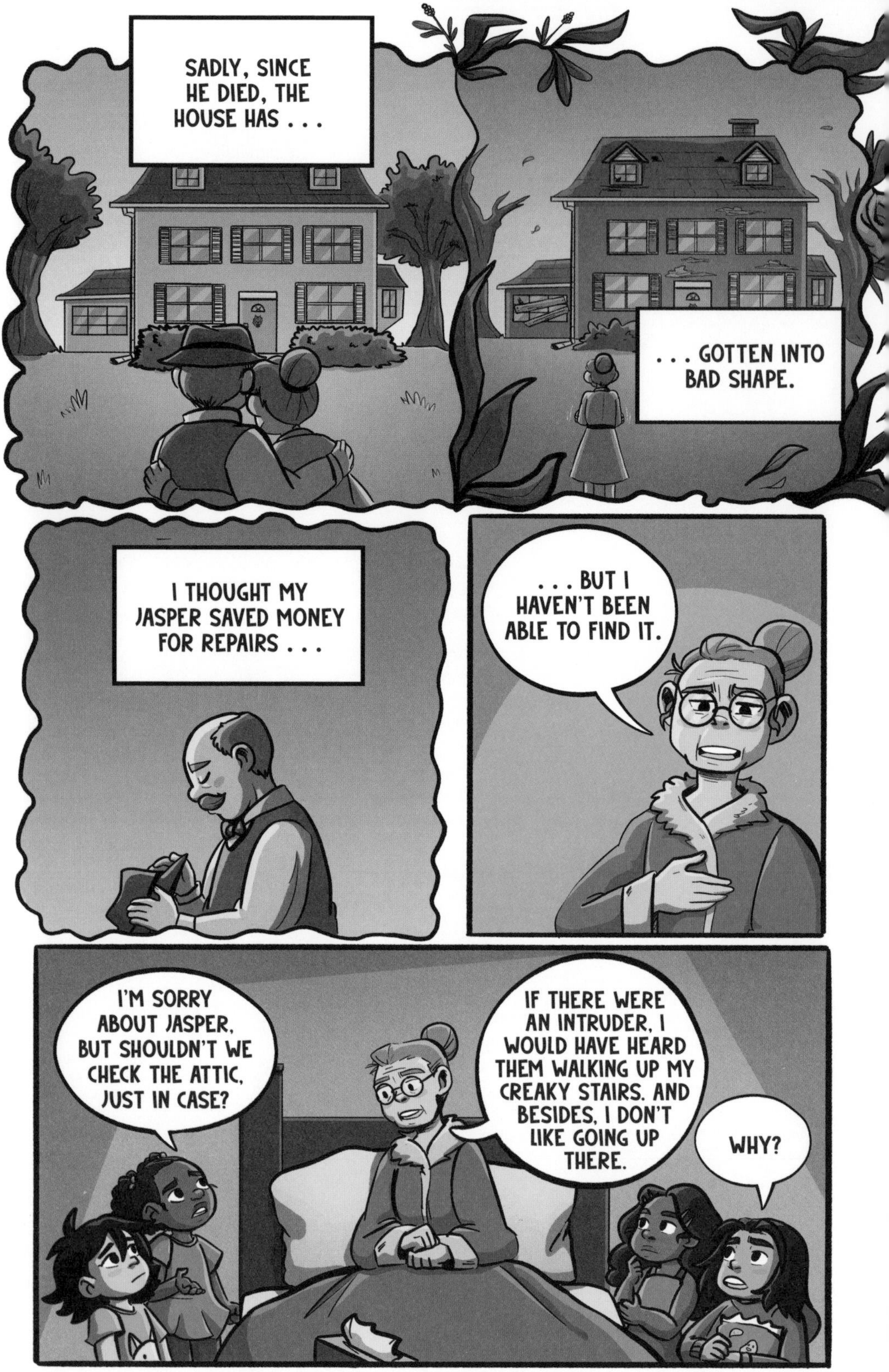
SADLY, SINCE HE DIED, THE HOUSE HAS . . .
. . . GOTTEN INTO BAD SHAPE.
I THOUGHT MY JASPER SAVED MONEY FOR REPAIRS . . .
. . . BUT I HAVEN'T BEEN ABLE TO FIND IT.
I'M SORRY ABOUT JASPER, BUT SHOULDN'T WE CHECK THE ATTIC, JUST IN CASE?
IF THERE WERE AN INTRUDER, I WOULD HAVE HEARD THEM WALKING UP MY CREAKY STAIRS. AND BESIDES, I DON'T LIKE GOING UP THERE.
WHY?

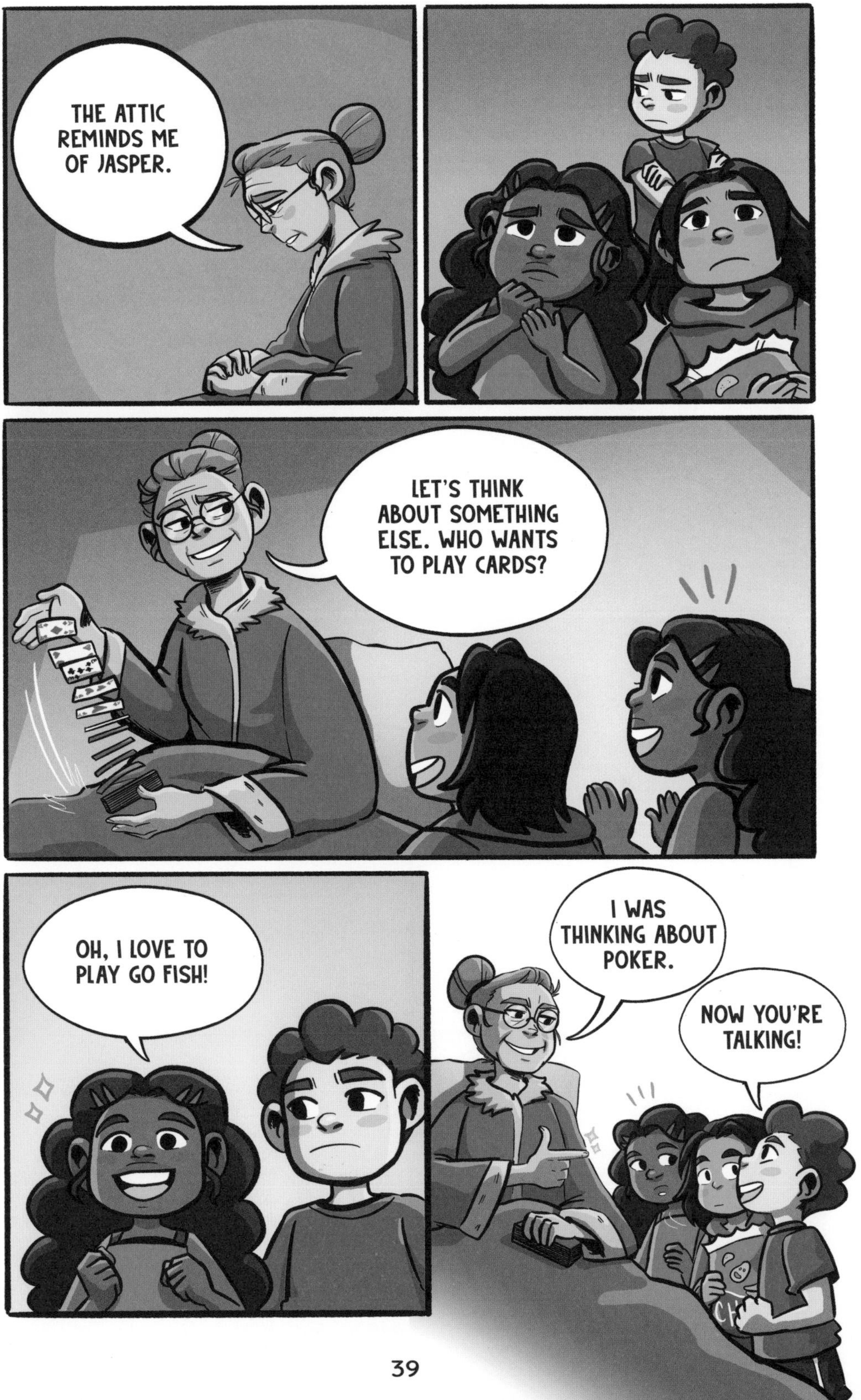
THE ATTIC REMINDS ME OF JASPER.
LET'S THINK ABOUT SOMETHING ELSE. WHO WANTS TO PLAY CARDS?
OH, I LOVE TO PLAY GO FISH!
I WAS THINKING ABOUT POKER.
NOW YOU'RE TALKING!

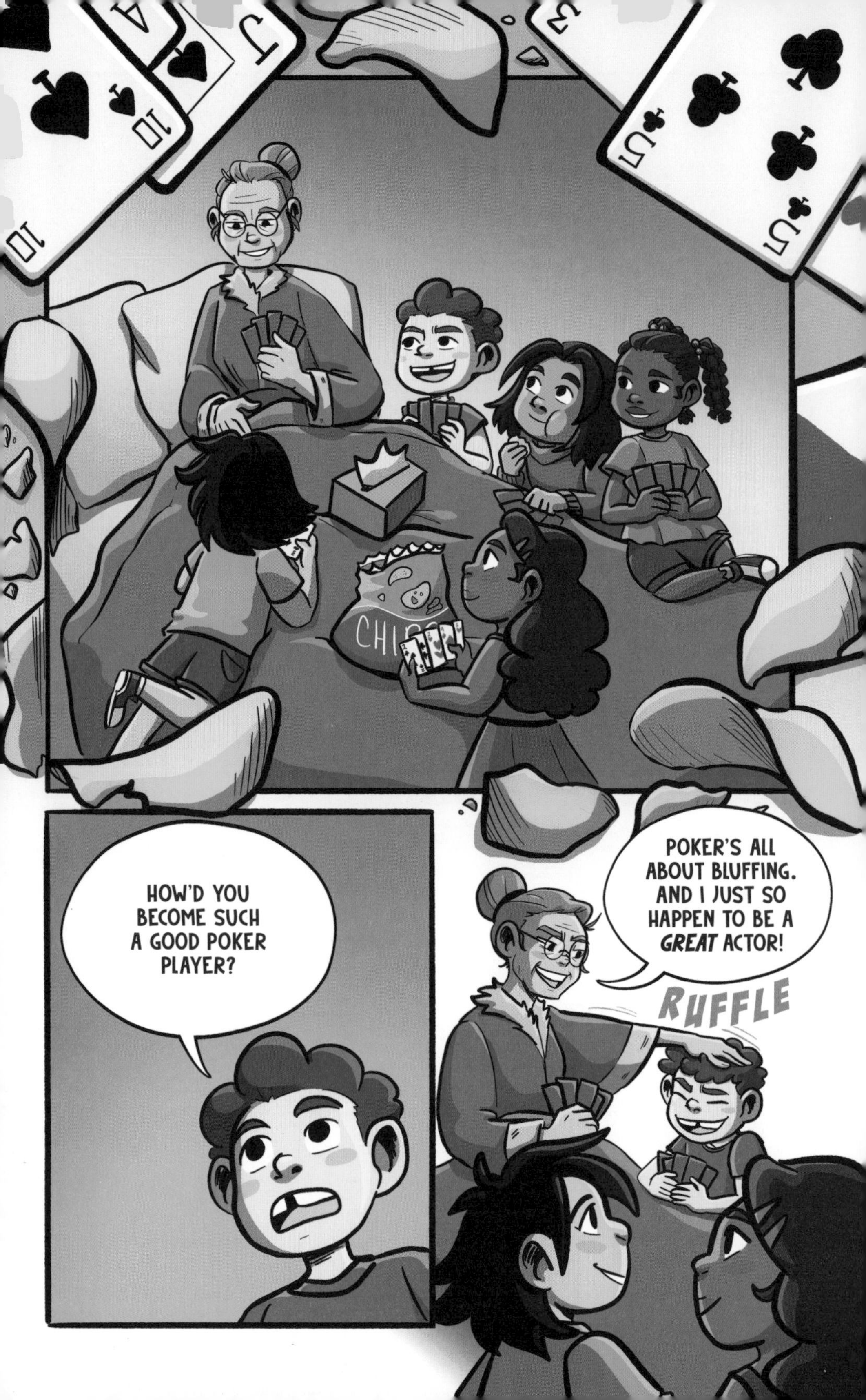
CHIPS
HOW'D YOU BECOME SUCH A GOOD POKER PLAYER?
POKER'S ALL ABOUT BLUFFING. AND I JUST SO HAPPEN TO BE A *GREAT* ACTOR!
RUFFLE

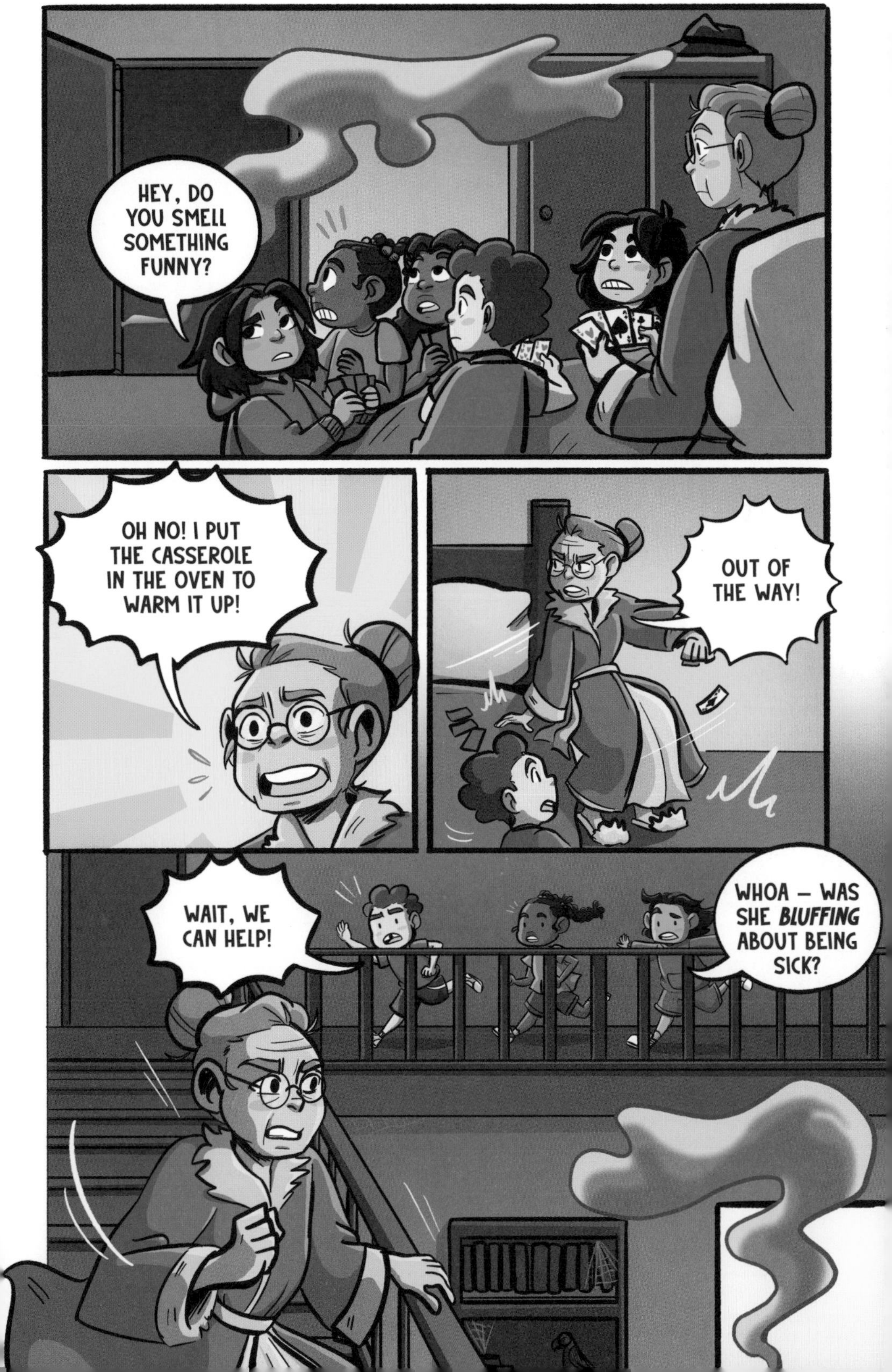
HEY, DO YOU SMELL SOMETHING FUNNY?
OH NO! I PUT THE CASSEROLE IN THE OVEN TO WARM IT UP!
OUT OF THE WAY!
WAIT, WE CAN HELP!
WHOA — WAS SHE *BLUFFING* ABOUT BEING SICK?

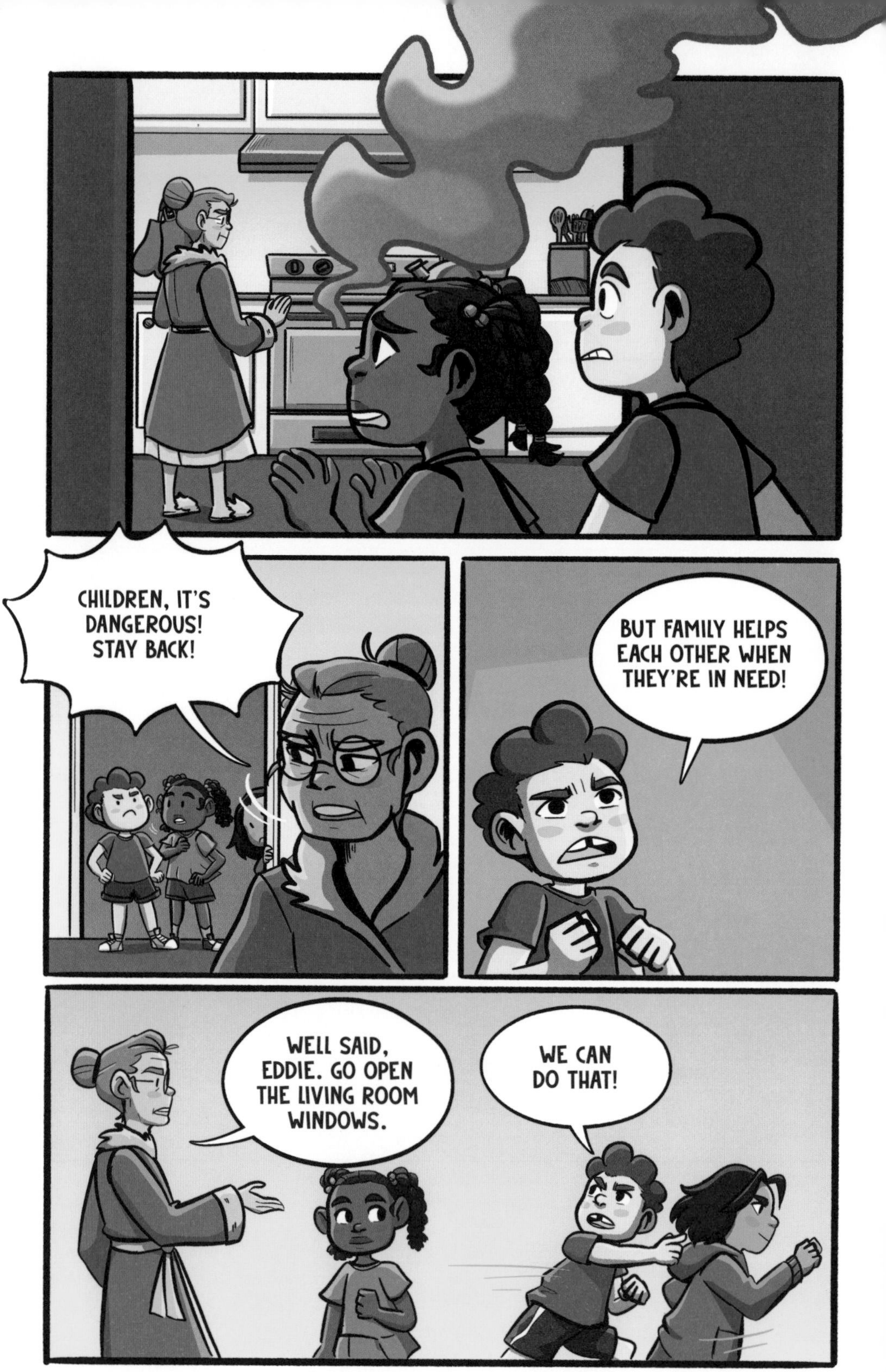
CHILDREN, IT'S DANGEROUS! STAY BACK!
BUT FAMILY HELPS EACH OTHER WHEN THEY'RE IN NEED!
WELL SAID, EDDIE. GO OPEN THE LIVING ROOM WINDOWS.
WE CAN DO THAT!

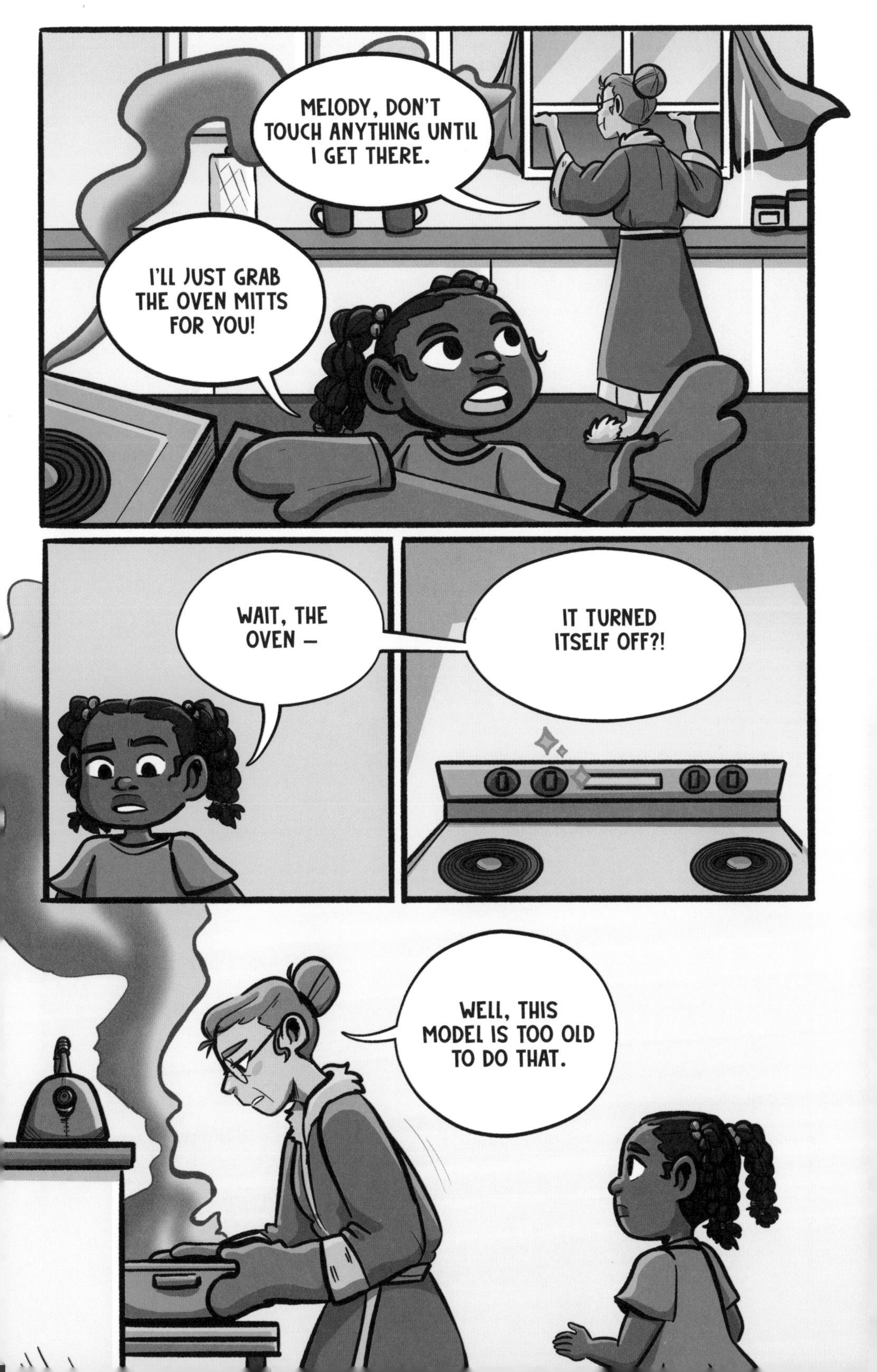
MELODY, DON'T TOUCH ANYTHING UNTIL I GET THERE.
I'LL JUST GRAB THE OVEN MITTS FOR YOU!
WAIT, THE OVEN –
IT TURNED ITSELF OFF?!
WELL, THIS MODEL IS TOO OLD TO DO THAT.

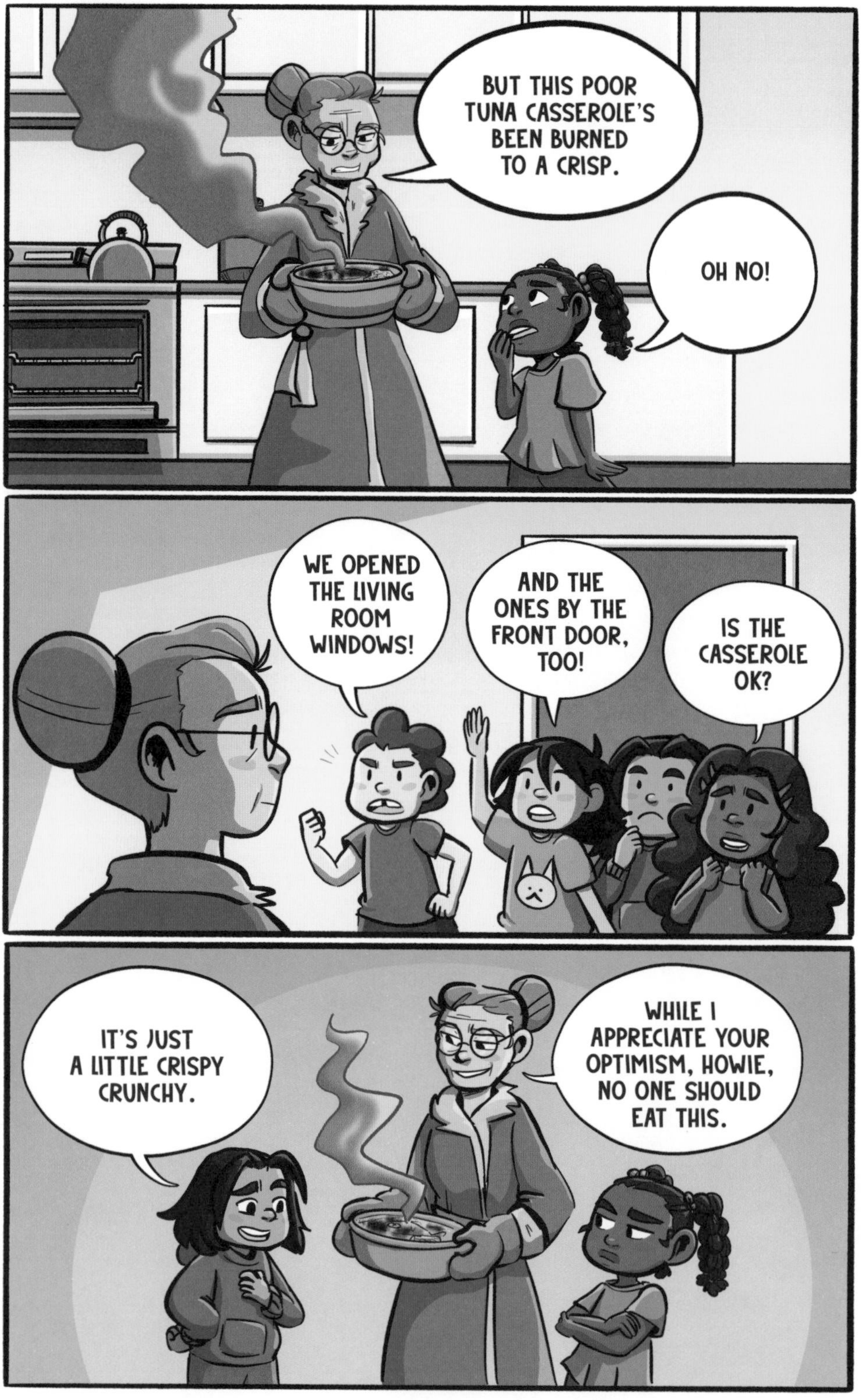
BUT THIS POOR TUNA CASSEROLE'S BEEN BURNED TO A CRISP.
OH NO!
WE OPENED THE LIVING ROOM WINDOWS!
AND THE ONES BY THE FRONT DOOR, TOO!
IS THE CASSEROLE OK?
IT'S JUST A LITTLE CRISPY CRUNCHY.
WHILE I APPRECIATE YOUR OPTIMISM, HOWIE, NO ONE SHOULD EAT THIS.

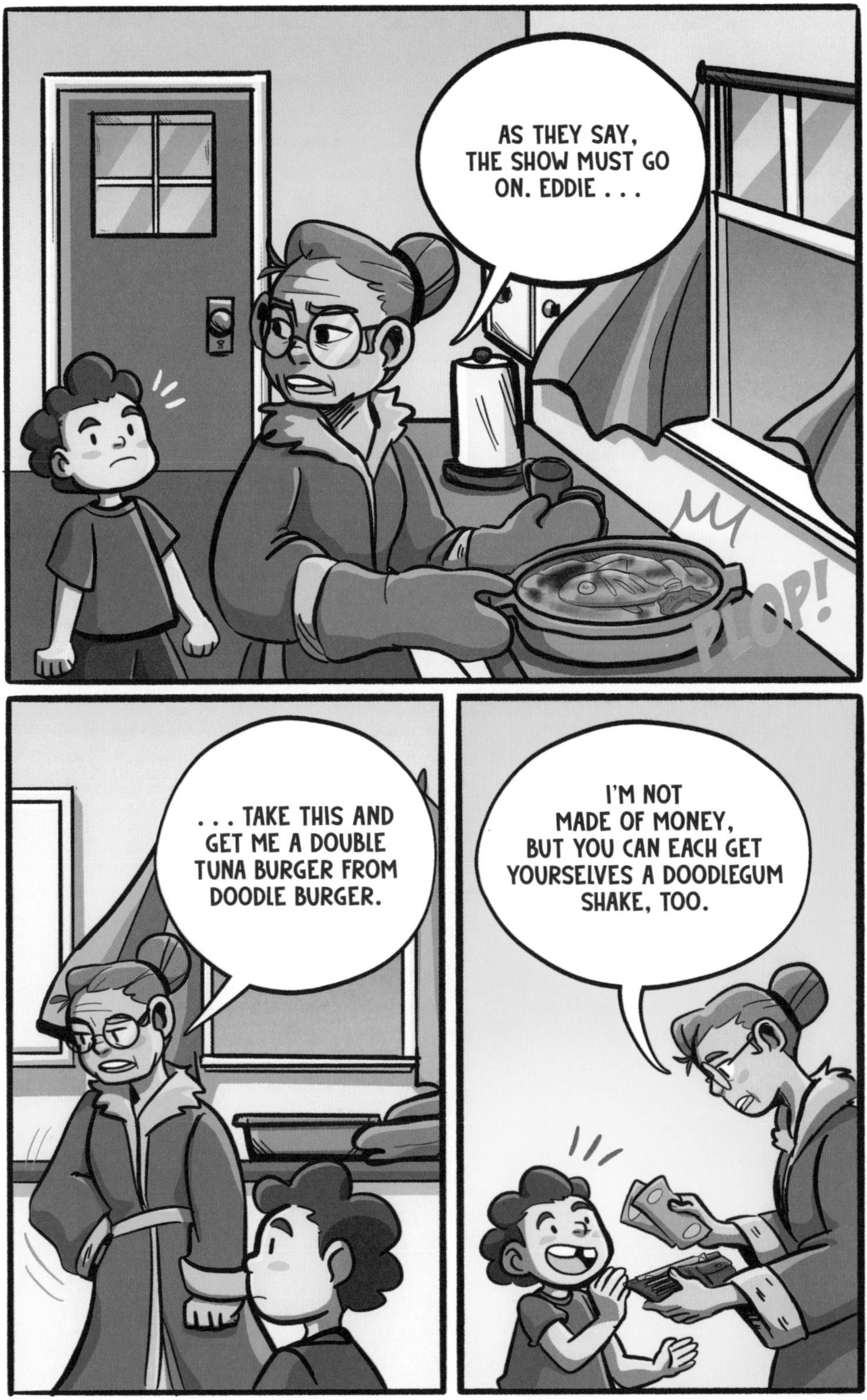
AS THEY SAY, THE SHOW MUST GO ON. EDDIE . . .
PLOP!
. . . TAKE THIS AND GET ME A DOUBLE TUNA BURGER FROM DOODLE BURGER.
I'M NOT MADE OF MONEY, BUT YOU CAN EACH GET YOURSELVES A DOODLEGUM SHAKE, TOO.

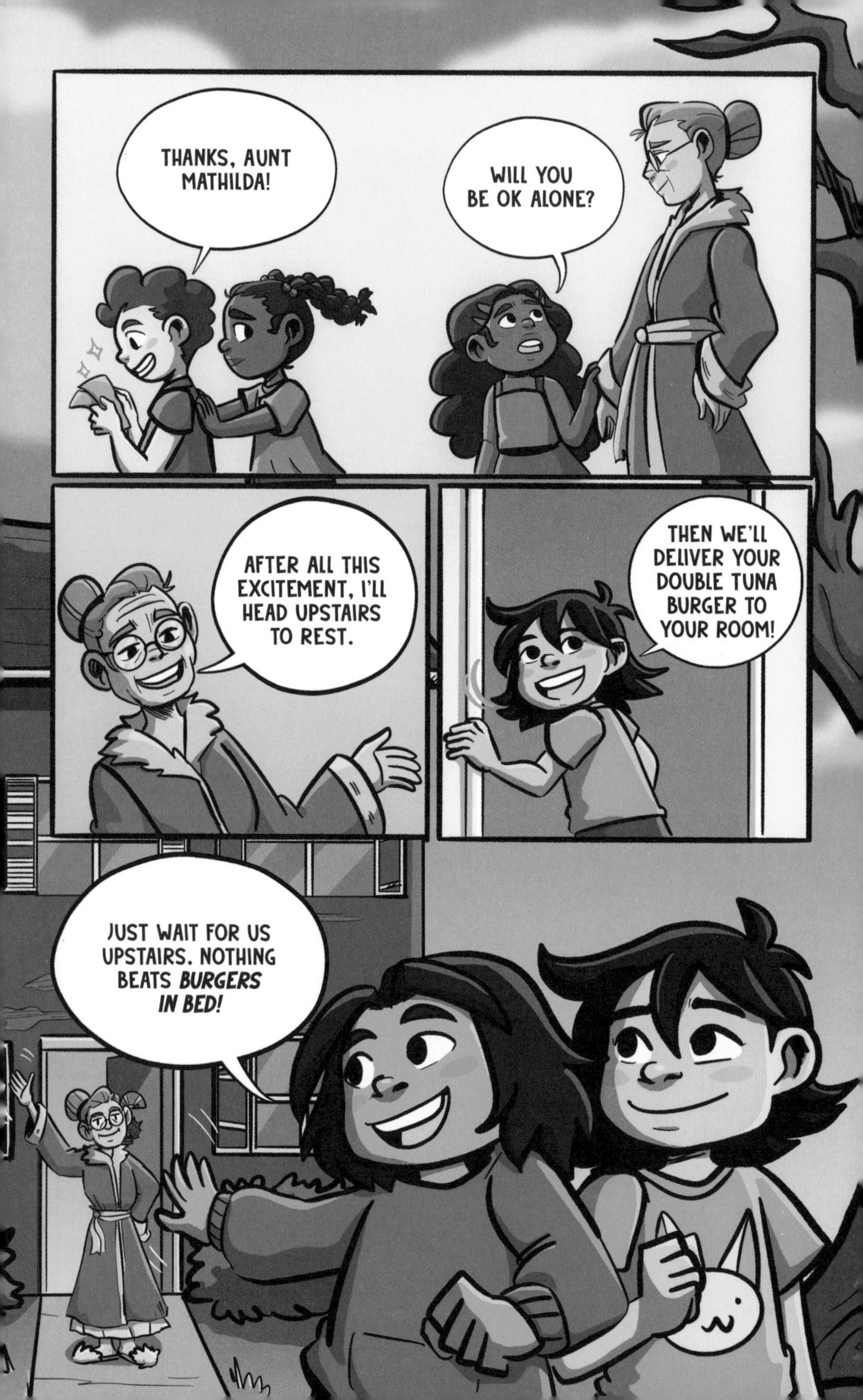
THANKS, AUNT MATHILDA!
WILL YOU BE OK ALONE?
AFTER ALL THIS EXCITEMENT, I'LL HEAD UPSTAIRS TO REST.
THEN WE'LL DELIVER YOUR DOUBLE TUNA BURGER TO YOUR ROOM!
JUST WAIT FOR US UPSTAIRS. NOTHING BEATS *BURGERS IN BED!*

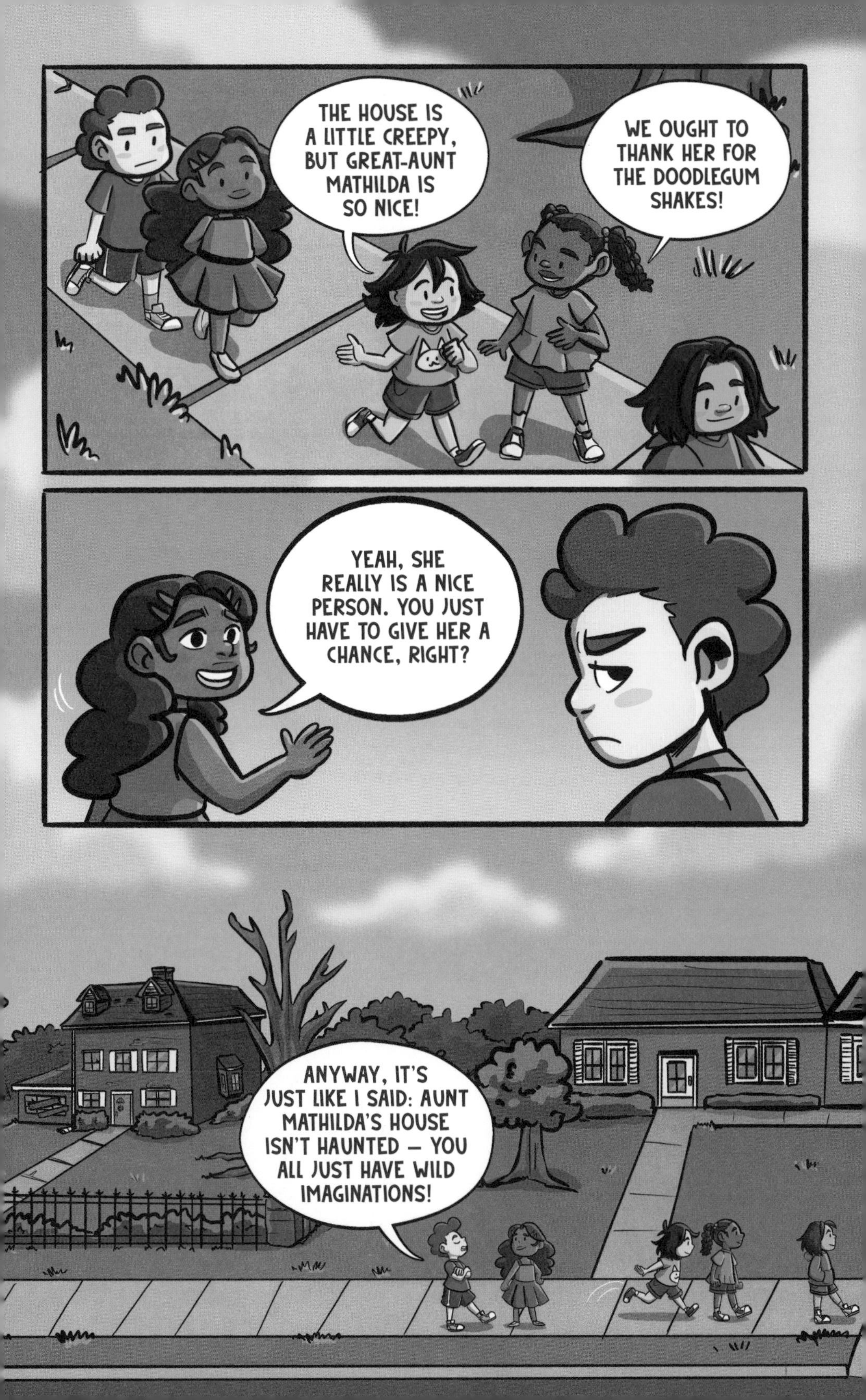
THE HOUSE IS A LITTLE CREEPY, BUT GREAT-AUNT MATHILDA IS SO NICE!
WE OUGHT TO THANK HER FOR THE DOODLEGUM SHAKES!
YEAH, SHE REALLY IS A NICE PERSON. YOU JUST HAVE TO GIVE HER A CHANCE, RIGHT?
ANYWAY, IT'S JUST LIKE I SAID: AUNT MATHILDA'S HOUSE ISN'T HAUNTED — YOU ALL JUST HAVE WILD IMAGINATIONS!

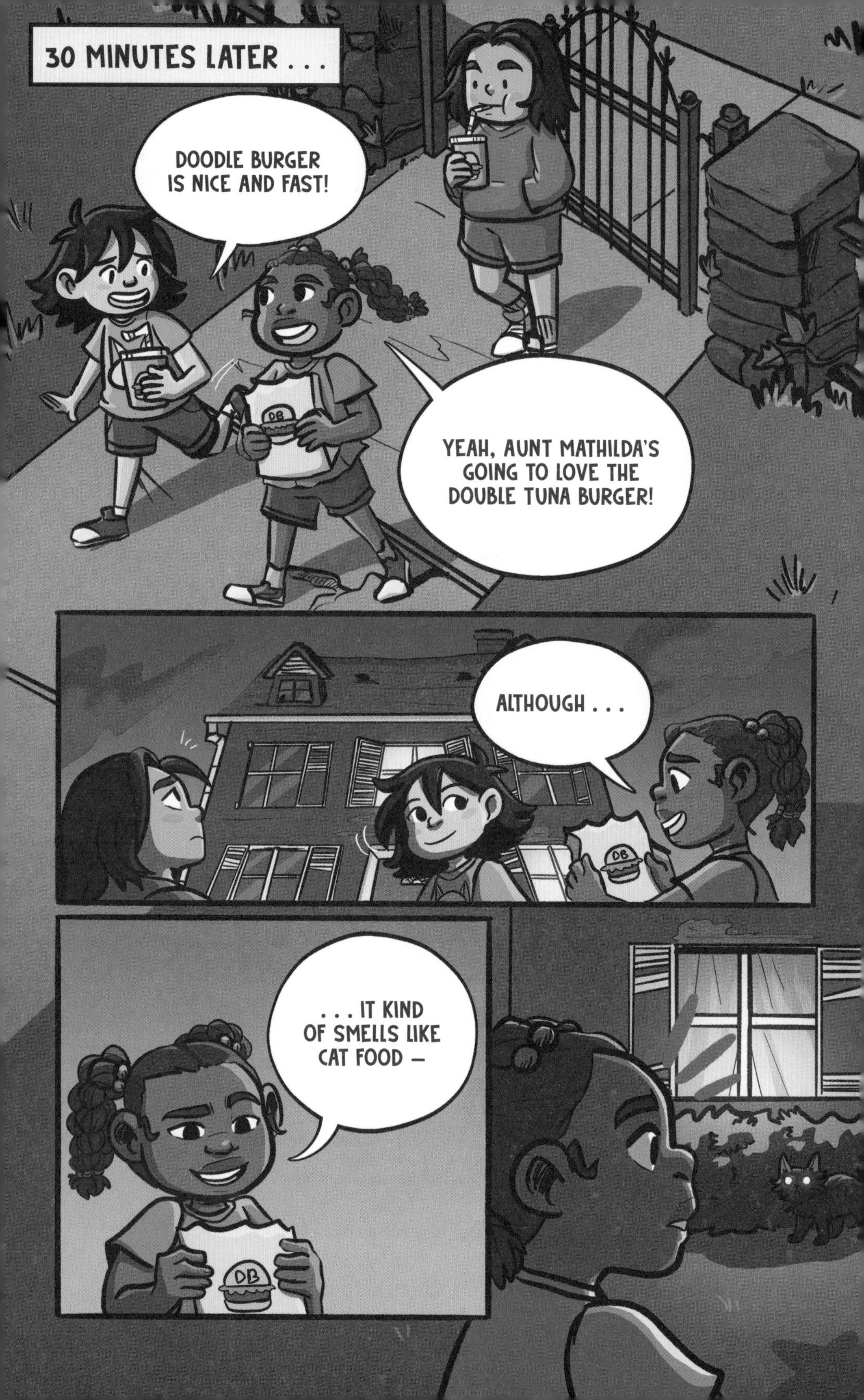
30 MINUTES LATER . . .
DOODLE BURGER IS NICE AND FAST!
YEAH, AUNT MATHILDA'S GOING TO LOVE THE DOUBLE TUNA BURGER!
ALTHOUGH . . .
. . . IT KIND OF SMELLS LIKE CAT FOOD —

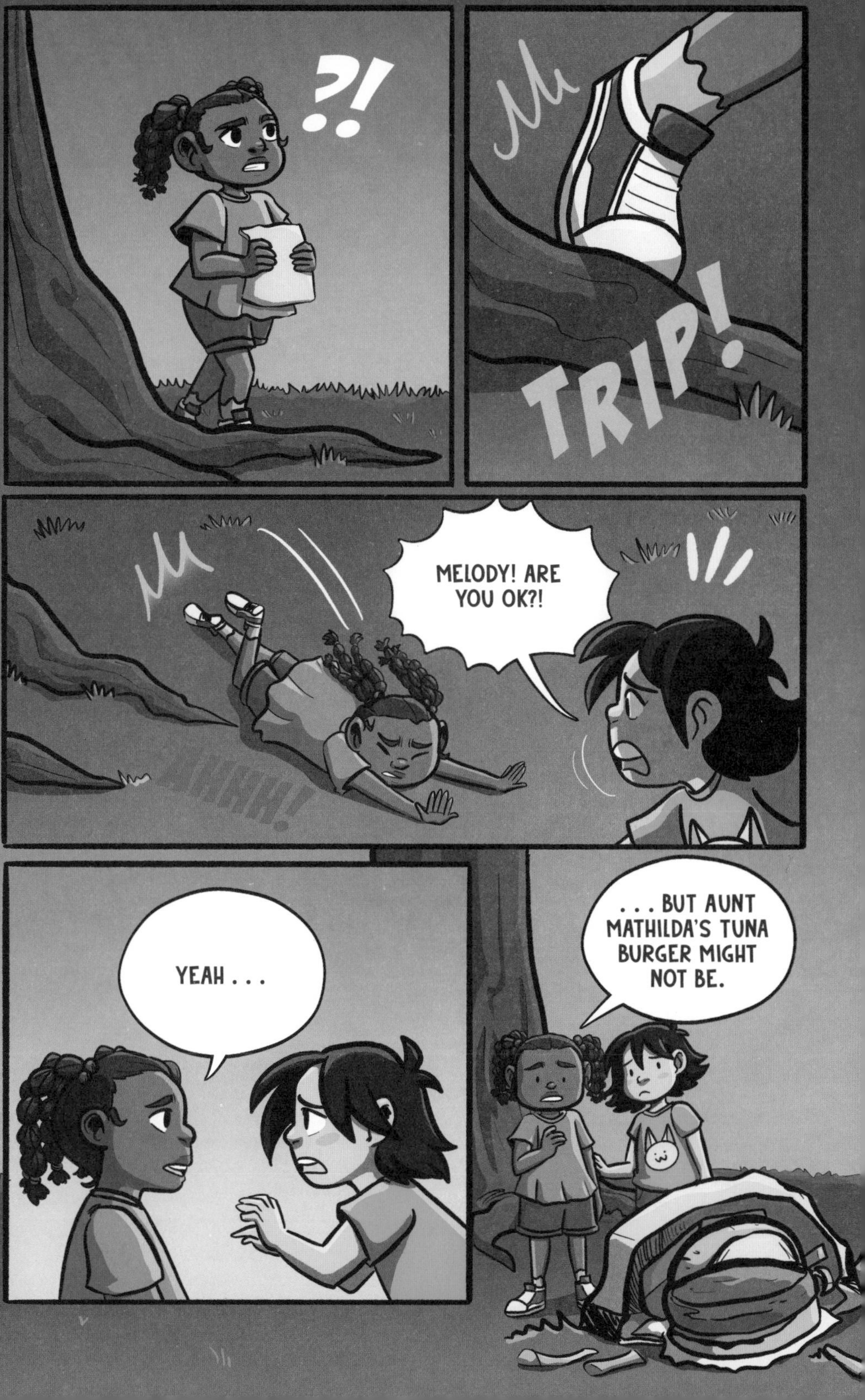
?!
TRIP!
MELODY! ARE YOU OK?!
YEAH . . .
. . . BUT AUNT MATHILDA'S TUNA BURGER MIGHT NOT BE.

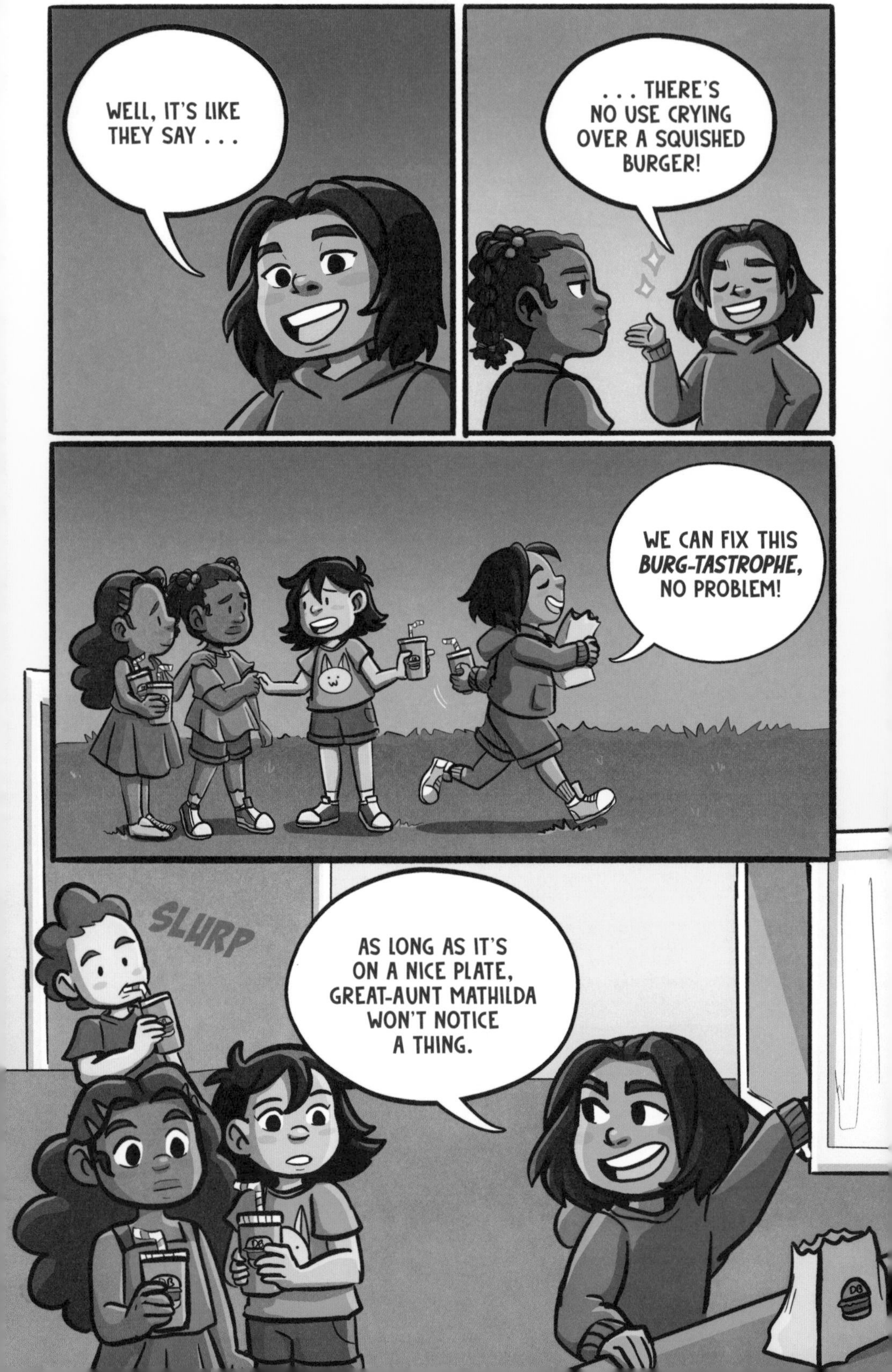
WELL, IT'S LIKE THEY SAY . . .
. . . THERE'S NO USE CRYING OVER A SQUISHED BURGER!
WE CAN FIX THIS *BURG-TASTROPHE*, NO PROBLEM!
SLURP
AS LONG AS IT'S ON A NICE PLATE, GREAT-AUNT MATHILDA WON'T NOTICE A THING.

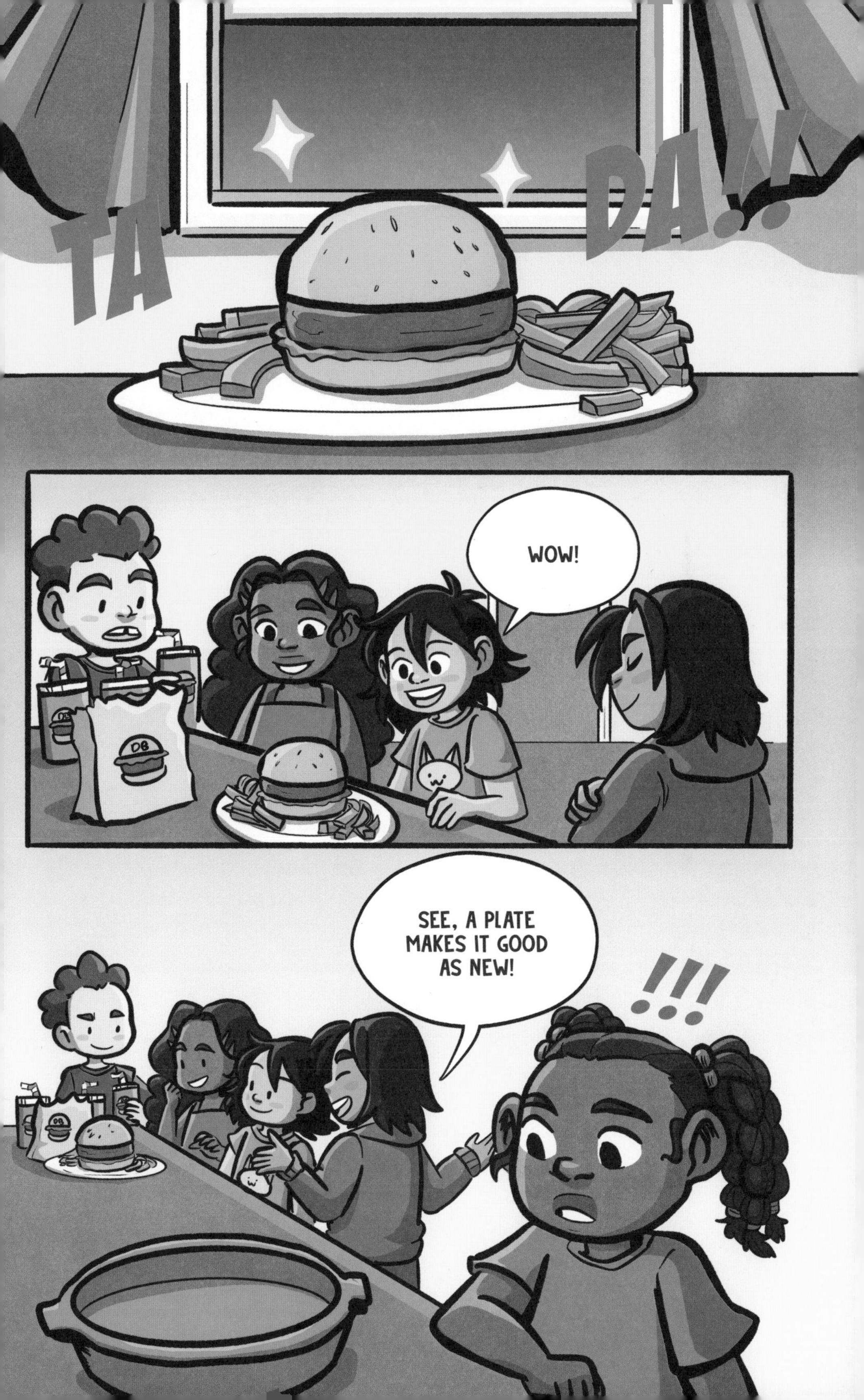
TA DA!!!
WOW!
SEE, A PLATE MAKES IT GOOD AS NEW!
!!!

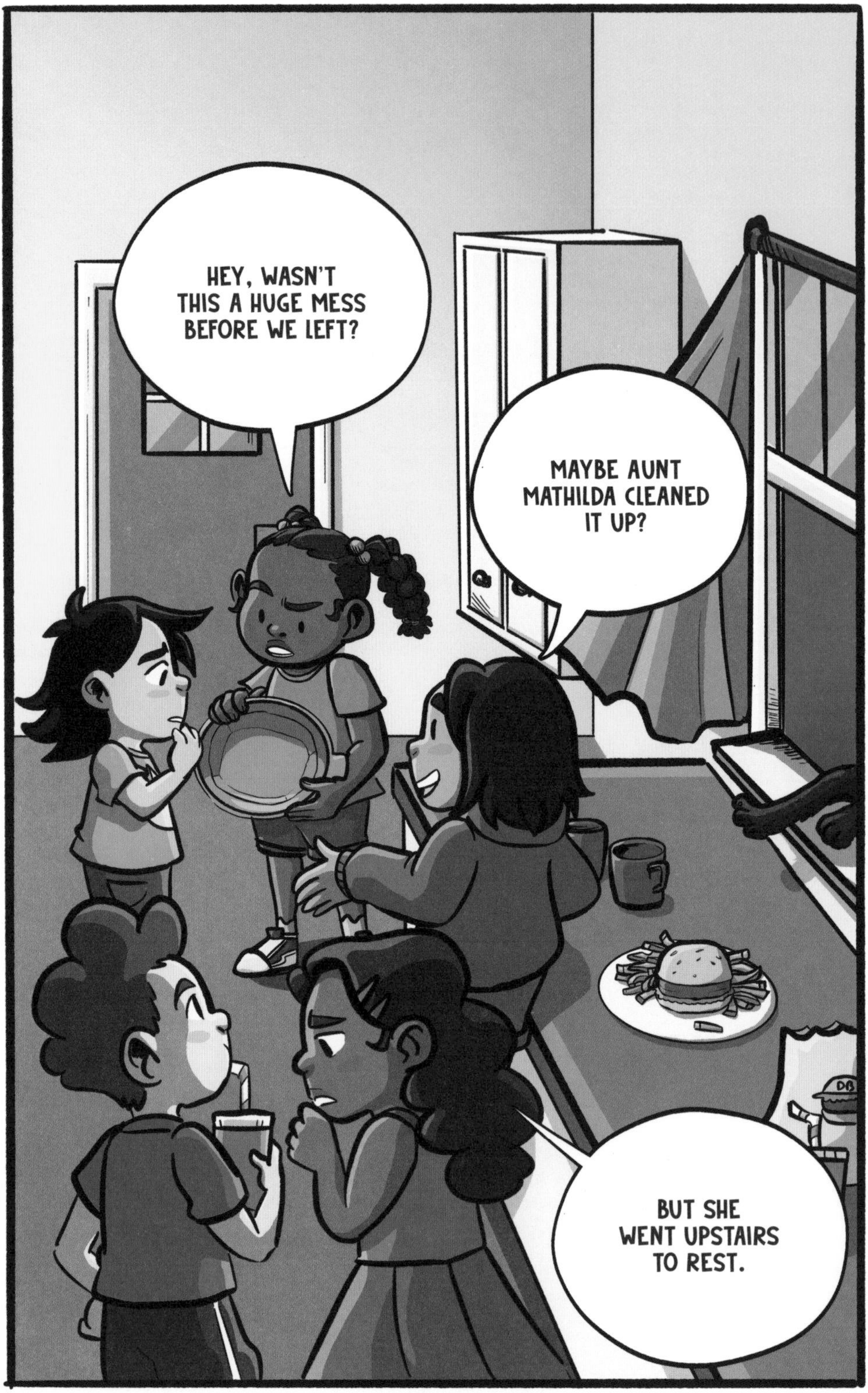
HEY, WASN'T THIS A HUGE MESS BEFORE WE LEFT?
MAYBE AUNT MATHILDA CLEANED IT UP?
BUT SHE WENT UPSTAIRS TO REST.

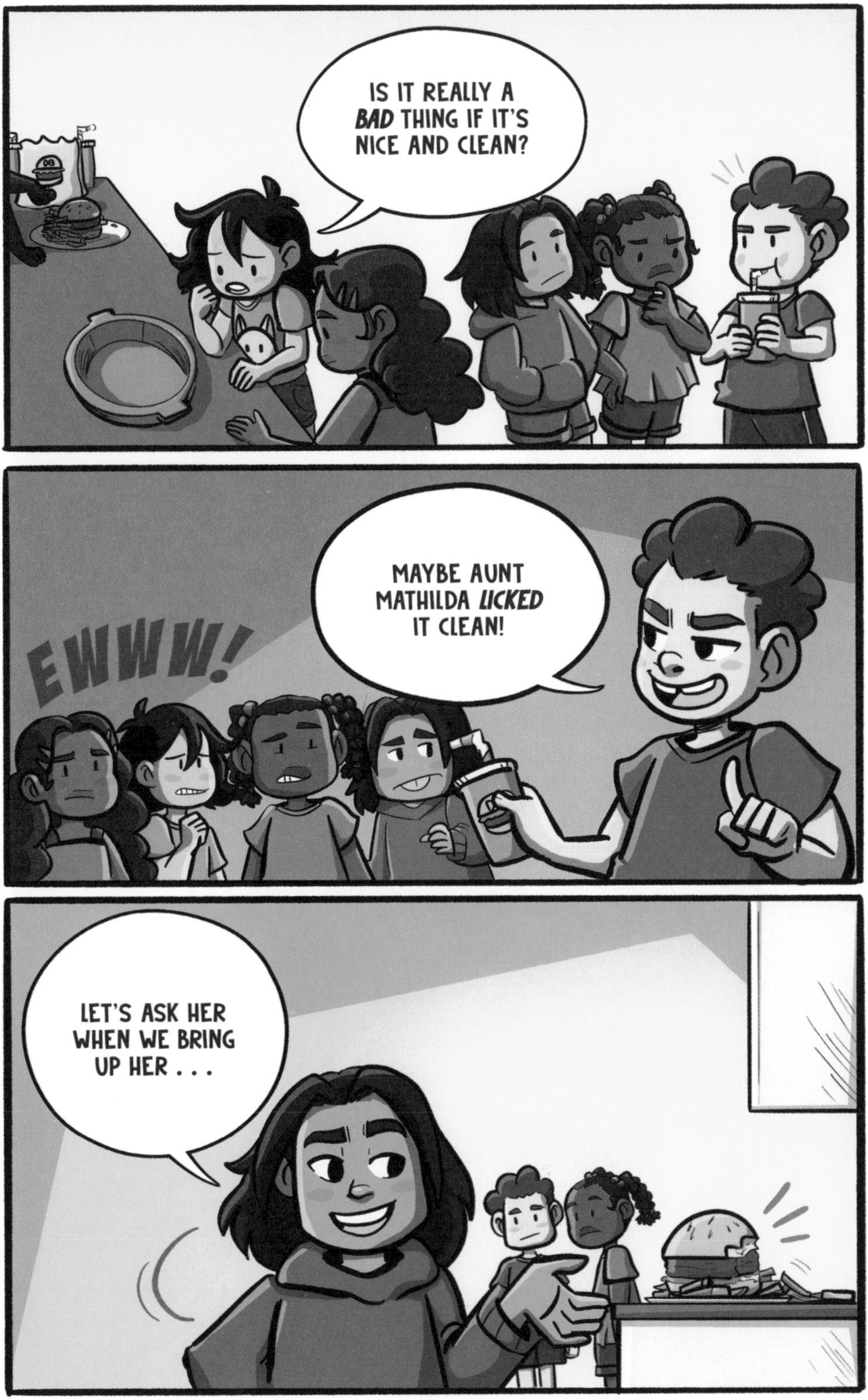
IS IT REALLY A *BAD* THING IF IT'S NICE AND CLEAN?
MAYBE AUNT MATHILDA *LICKED* IT CLEAN!
EWWW!
LET'S ASK HER WHEN WE BRING UP HER . . .

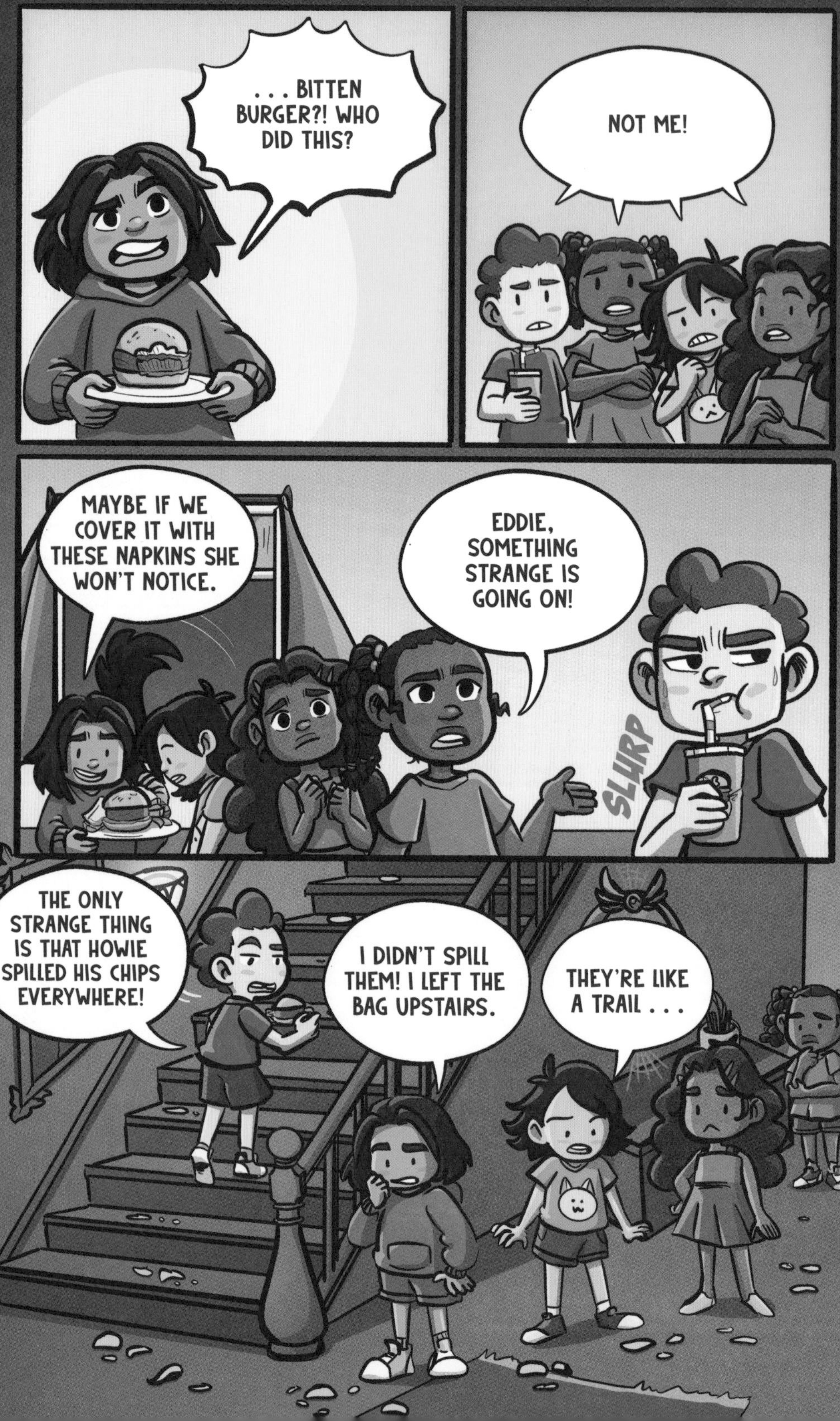
. . . BITTEN BURGER?! WHO DID THIS?
NOT ME!
MAYBE IF WE COVER IT WITH THESE NAPKINS SHE WON'T NOTICE.
EDDIE, SOMETHING STRANGE IS GOING ON!
SLURP
THE ONLY STRANGE THING IS THAT HOWIE SPILLED HIS CHIPS EVERYWHERE!
I DIDN'T SPILL THEM! I LEFT THE BAG UPSTAIRS.
THEY'RE LIKE A TRAIL . . .

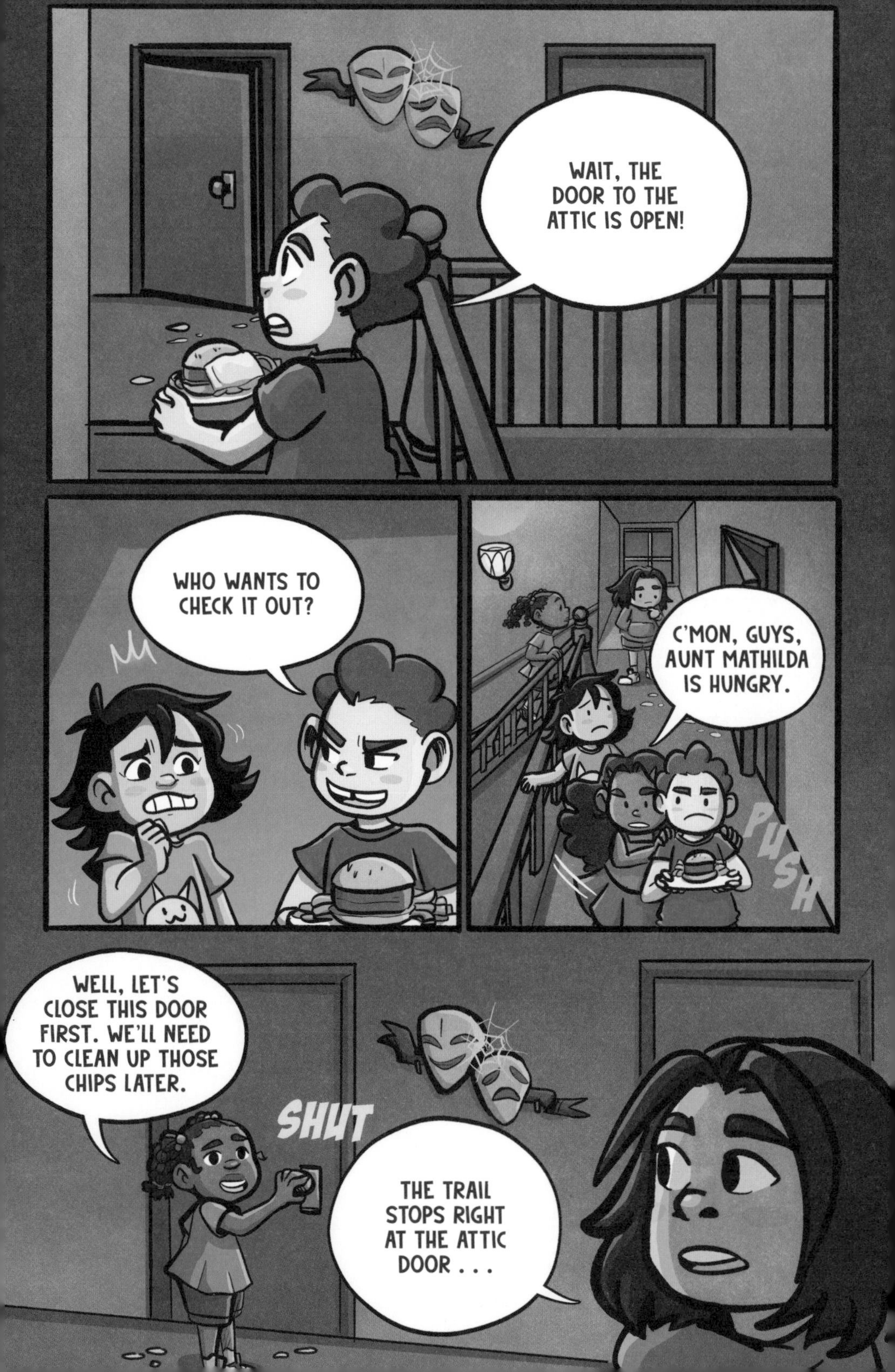
WAIT, THE DOOR TO THE ATTIC IS OPEN!
WHO WANTS TO CHECK IT OUT?
C'MON, GUYS, AUNT MATHILDA IS HUNGRY.
PUSH
WELL, LET'S CLOSE THIS DOOR FIRST. WE'LL NEED TO CLEAN UP THOSE CHIPS LATER.
SHUT
THE TRAIL STOPS RIGHT AT THE ATTIC DOOR . . .

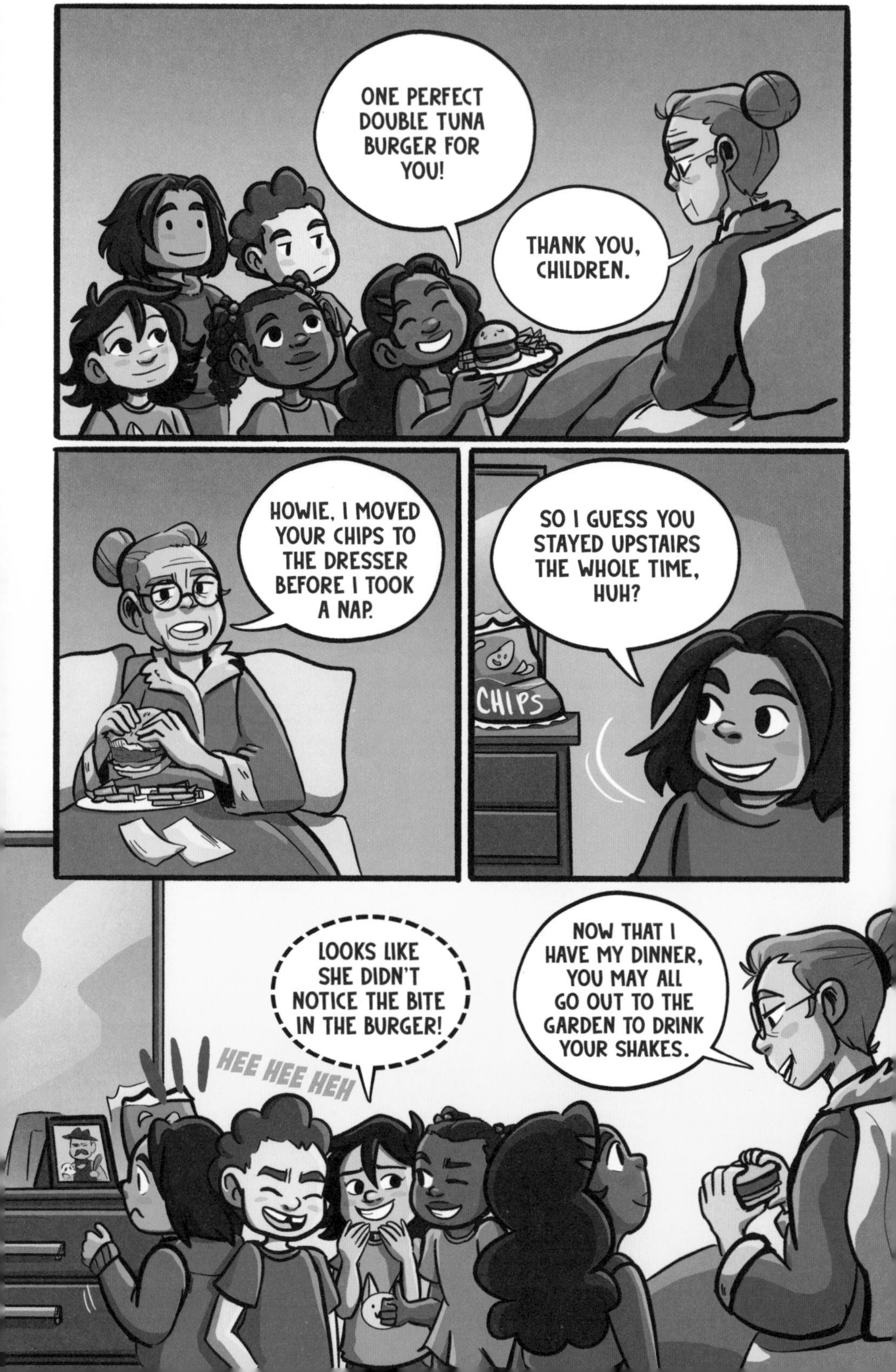
ONE PERFECT DOUBLE TUNA BURGER FOR YOU!
THANK YOU, CHILDREN.
HOWIE, I MOVED YOUR CHIPS TO THE DRESSER BEFORE I TOOK A NAP.
SO I GUESS YOU STAYED UPSTAIRS THE WHOLE TIME, HUH?
CHIPS
LOOKS LIKE SHE DIDN'T NOTICE THE BITE IN THE BURGER!
HEE HEE HEH
NOW THAT I HAVE MY DINNER, YOU MAY ALL GO OUT TO THE GARDEN TO DRINK YOUR SHAKES.

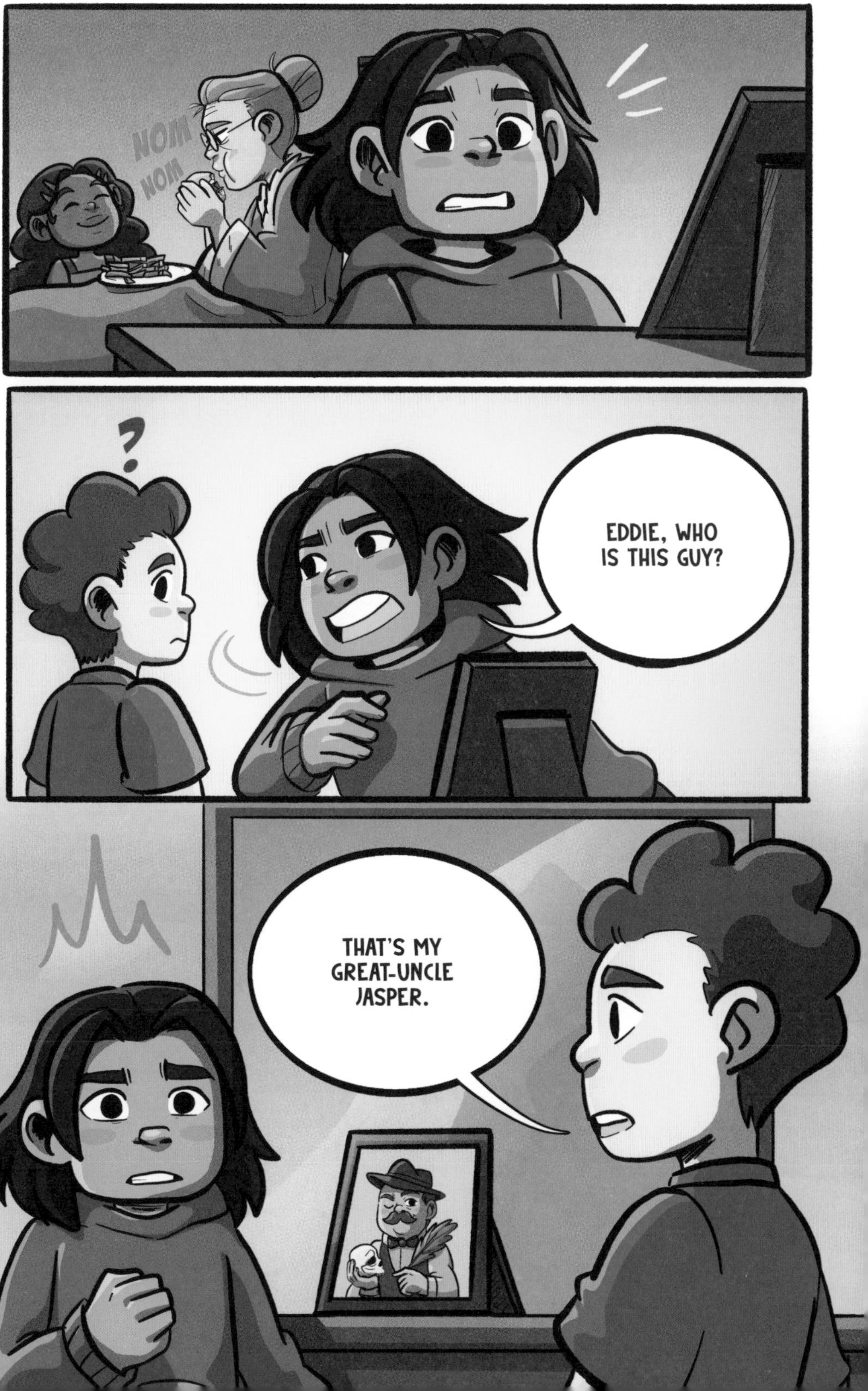
NOM NOM
EDDIE, WHO IS THIS GUY?
THAT'S MY GREAT-UNCLE JASPER.

CHAPTER 4 THE ATTIC

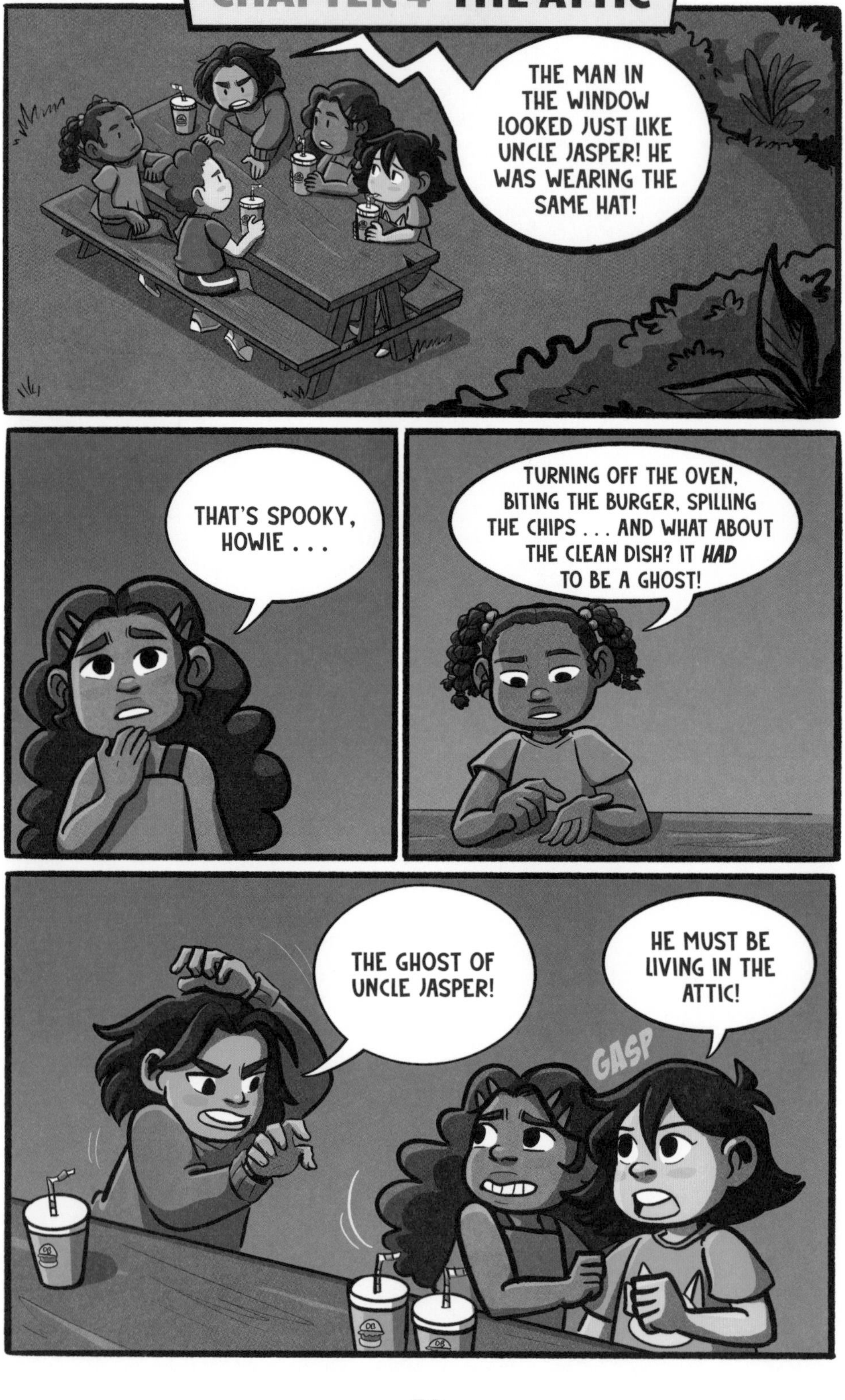
THE MAN IN THE WINDOW LOOKED JUST LIKE UNCLE JASPER! HE WAS WEARING THE SAME HAT!
THAT'S SPOOKY, HOWIE . . .
TURNING OFF THE OVEN, BITING THE BURGER, SPILLING THE CHIPS . . . AND WHAT ABOUT THE CLEAN DISH? IT *HAD* TO BE A GHOST!
THE GHOST OF UNCLE JASPER!
HE MUST BE LIVING IN THE ATTIC!
GASP

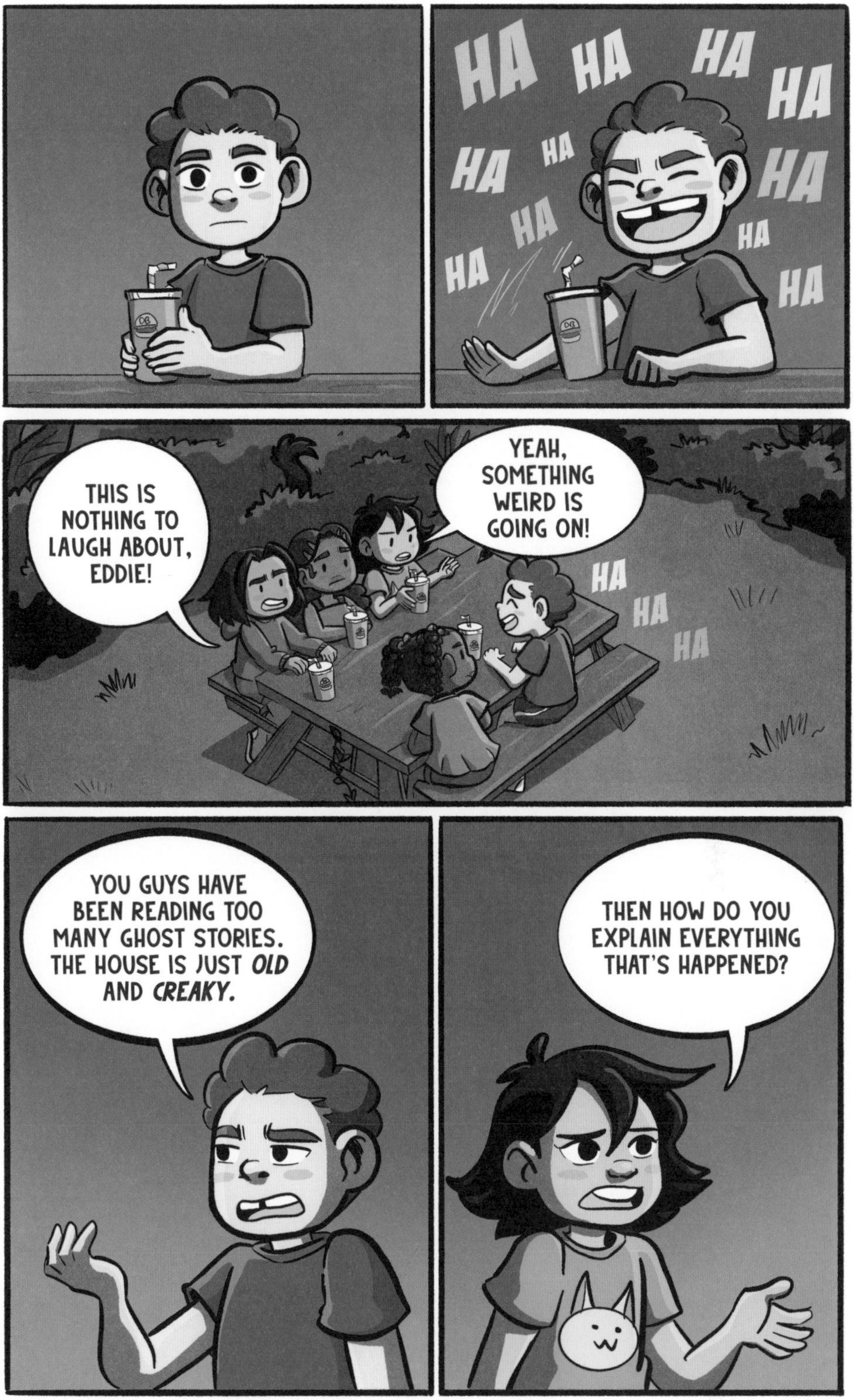
HA HA HA HA HA HA HA HA HA HA HA HA
THIS IS NOTHING TO LAUGH ABOUT, EDDIE!
YEAH, SOMETHING WEIRD IS GOING ON!
HA HA HA
YOU GUYS HAVE BEEN READING TOO MANY GHOST STORIES. THE HOUSE IS JUST OLD AND CREAKY.
THEN HOW DO YOU EXPLAIN EVERYTHING THAT'S HAPPENED?

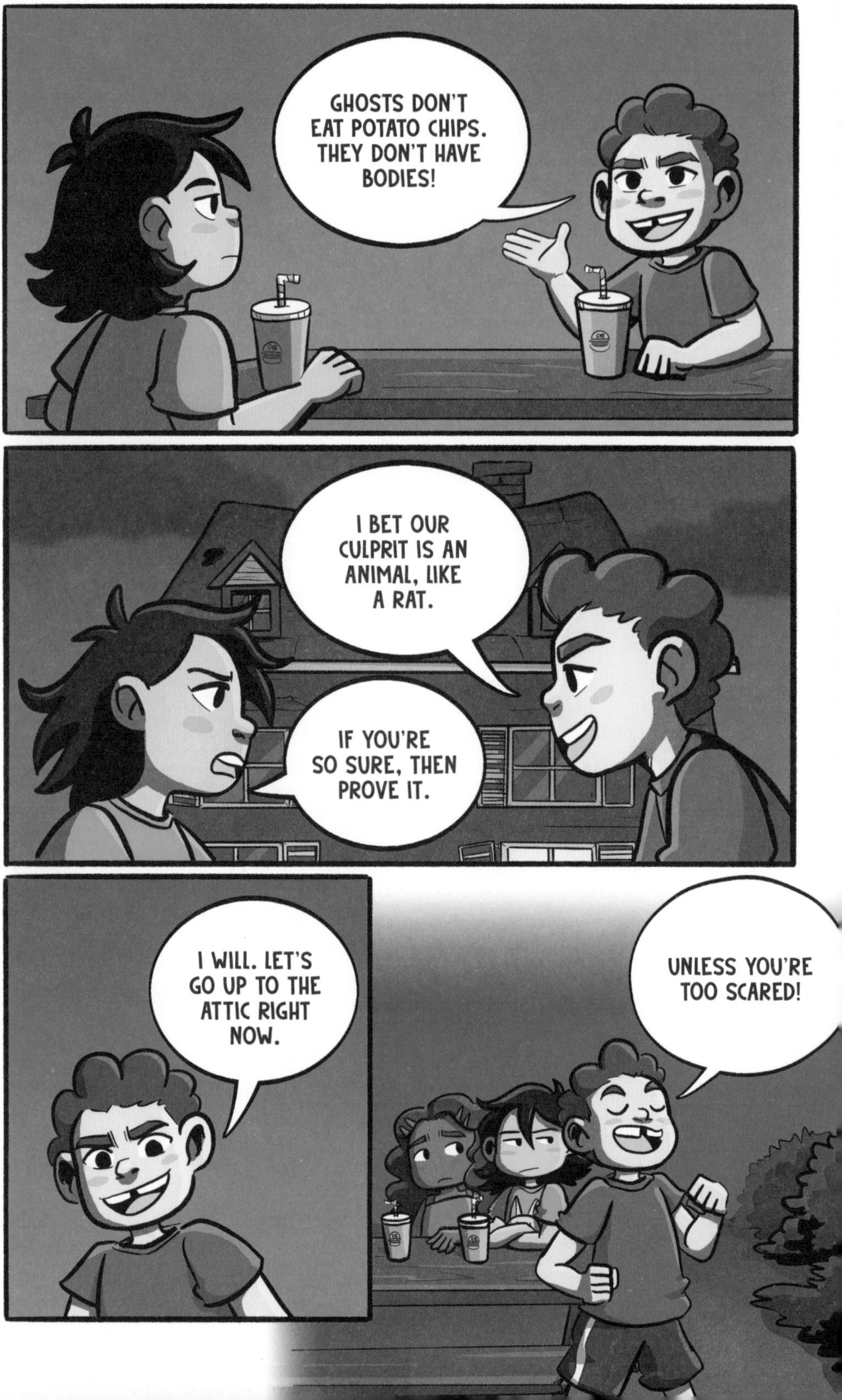
GHOSTS DON'T EAT POTATO CHIPS. THEY DON'T HAVE BODIES!
I BET OUR CULPRIT IS AN ANIMAL, LIKE A RAT.
IF YOU'RE SO SURE, THEN PROVE IT.
I WILL. LET'S GO UP TO THE ATTIC RIGHT NOW.
UNLESS YOU'RE TOO SCARED!

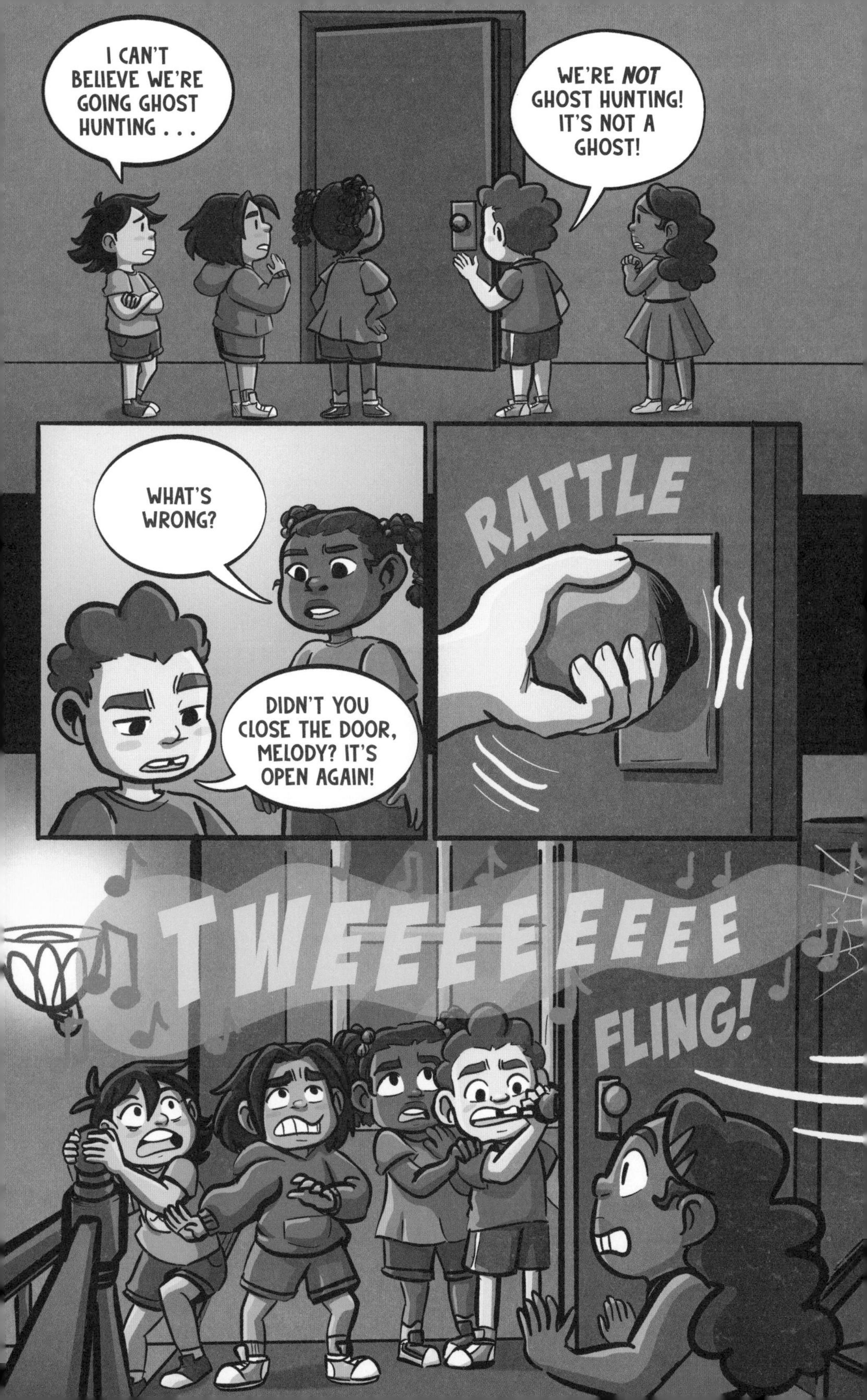
I CAN'T BELIEVE WE'RE GOING GHOST HUNTING . . .
WE'RE *NOT* GHOST HUNTING! IT'S NOT A GHOST!
WHAT'S WRONG?
DIDN'T YOU CLOSE THE DOOR, MELODY? IT'S OPEN AGAIN!
RATTLE
TWEEEEEEEE
FLING!

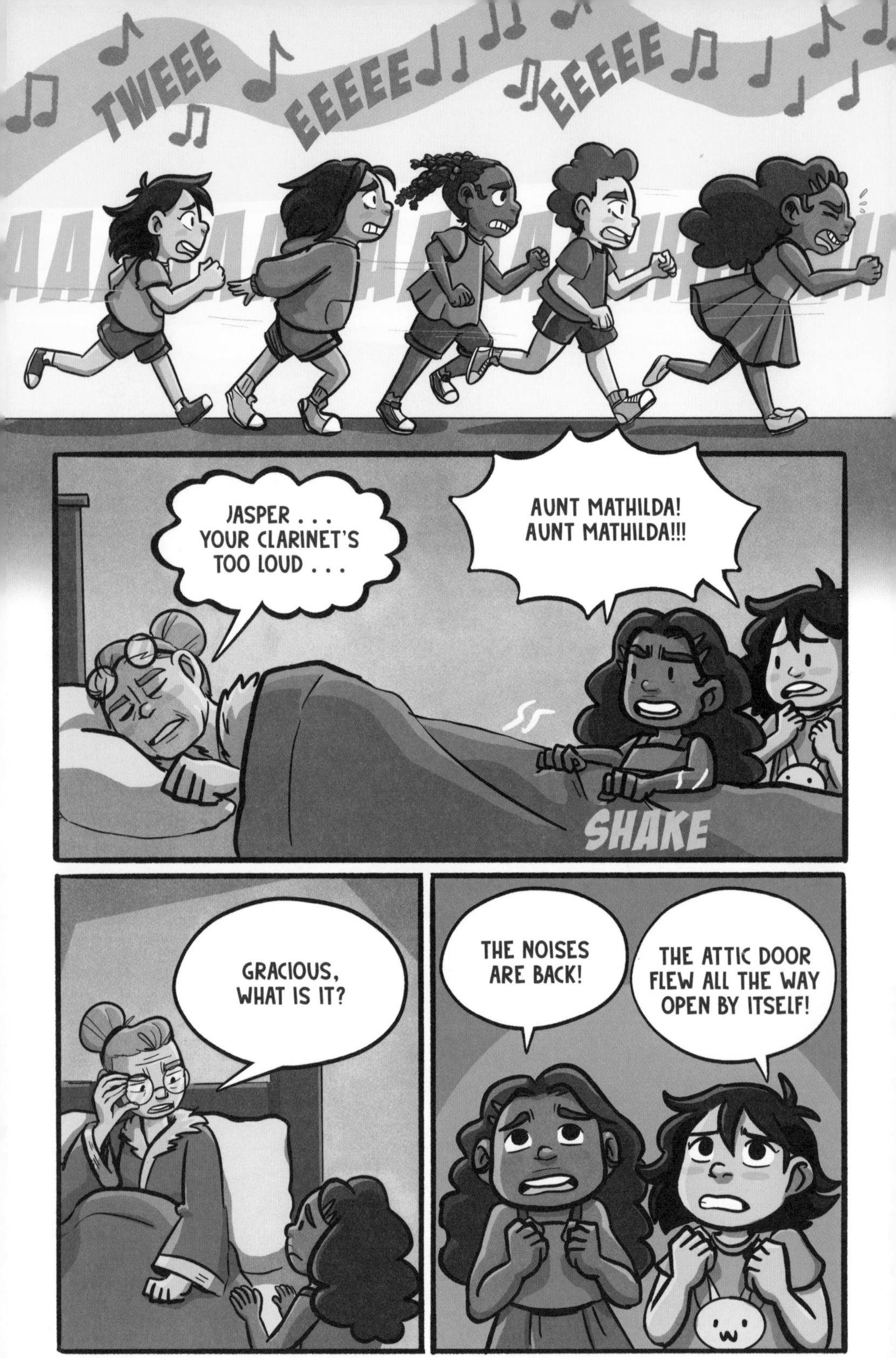
TWEEE
EEEEE
EEEEE
JASPER . . . YOUR CLARINET'S TOO LOUD . . .
AUNT MATHILDA! AUNT MATHILDA!!!
SHAKE
GRACIOUS, WHAT IS IT?
THE NOISES ARE BACK!
THE ATTIC DOOR FLEW ALL THE WAY OPEN BY ITSELF!

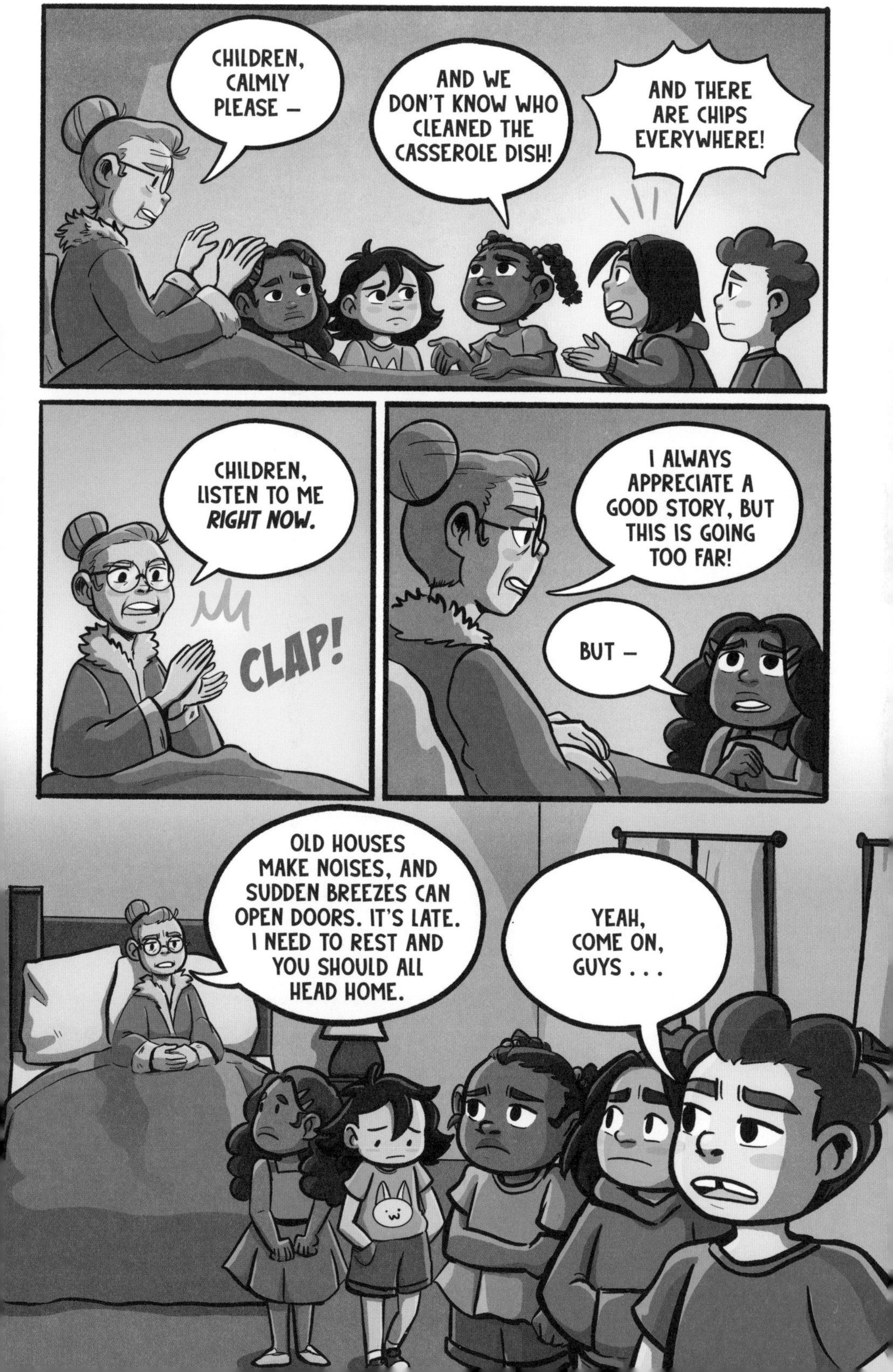
CHILDREN, CALMLY PLEASE –
AND WE DON'T KNOW WHO CLEANED THE CASSEROLE DISH!
AND THERE ARE CHIPS EVERYWHERE!
CHILDREN, LISTEN TO ME *RIGHT NOW.*
CLAP!
I ALWAYS APPRECIATE A GOOD STORY, BUT THIS IS GOING TOO FAR!
BUT –
OLD HOUSES MAKE NOISES, AND SUDDEN BREEZES CAN OPEN DOORS. IT'S LATE. I NEED TO REST AND YOU SHOULD ALL HEAD HOME.
YEAH, COME ON, GUYS . . .

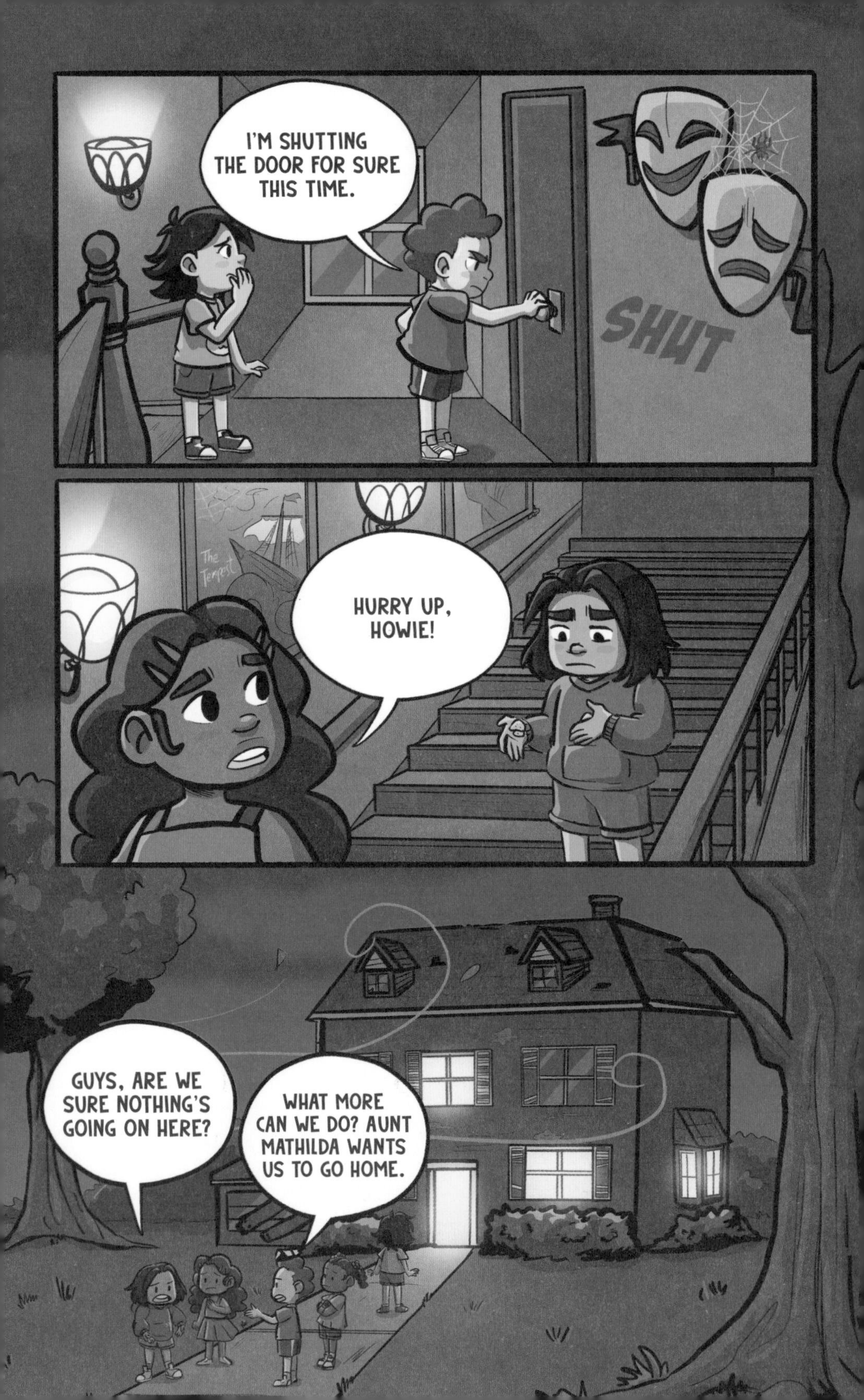
I'M SHUTTING THE DOOR FOR SURE THIS TIME.
SHUT
The Tempest
HURRY UP, HOWIE!
GUYS, ARE WE SURE NOTHING'S GOING ON HERE?
WHAT MORE CAN WE DO? AUNT MATHILDA WANTS US TO GO HOME.

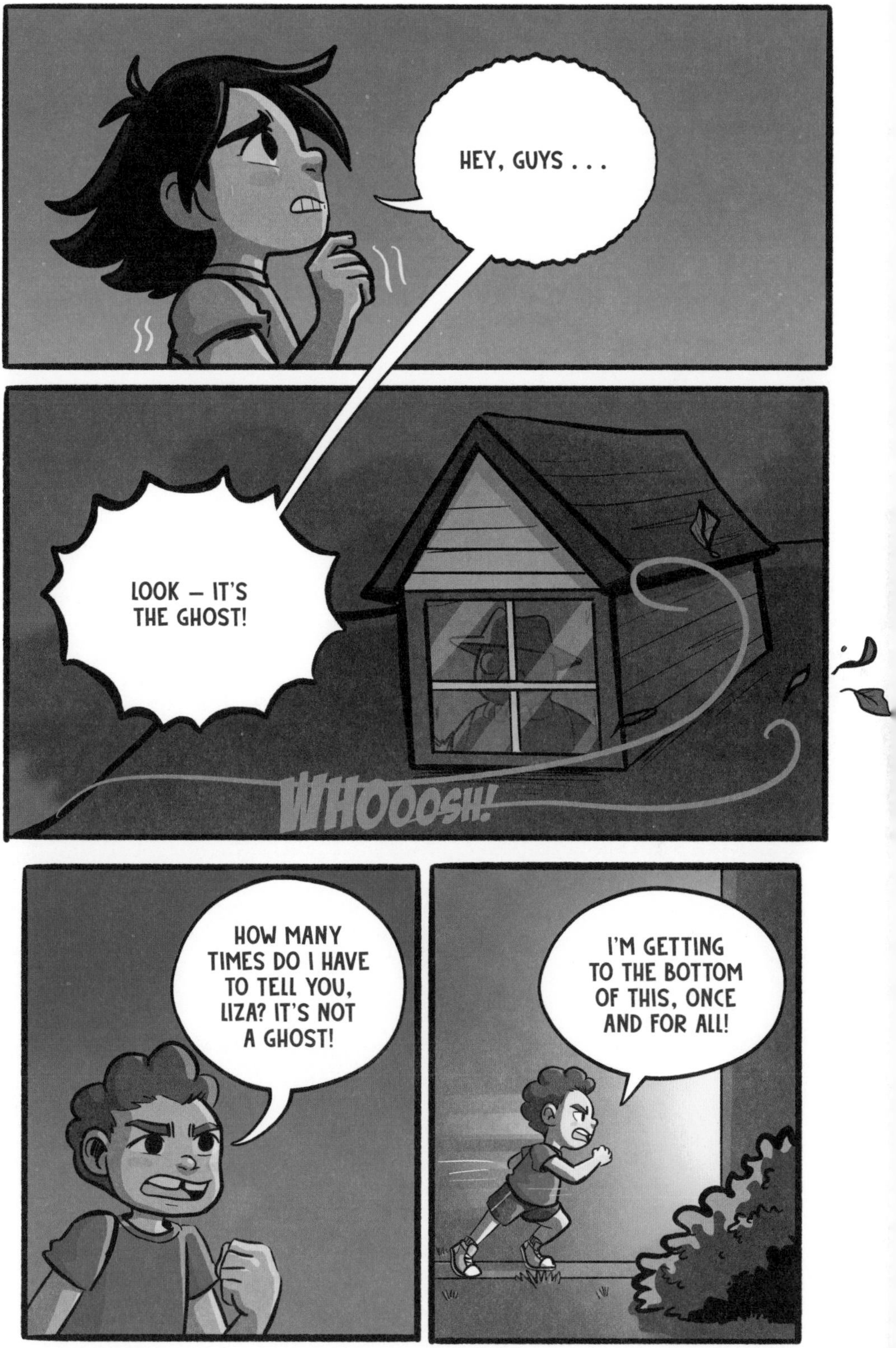
HEY, GUYS . . .
LOOK — IT'S THE GHOST!
WHOOOSH!
HOW MANY TIMES DO I HAVE TO TELL YOU, LIZA? IT'S NOT A GHOST!
I'M GETTING TO THE BOTTOM OF THIS, ONCE AND FOR ALL!

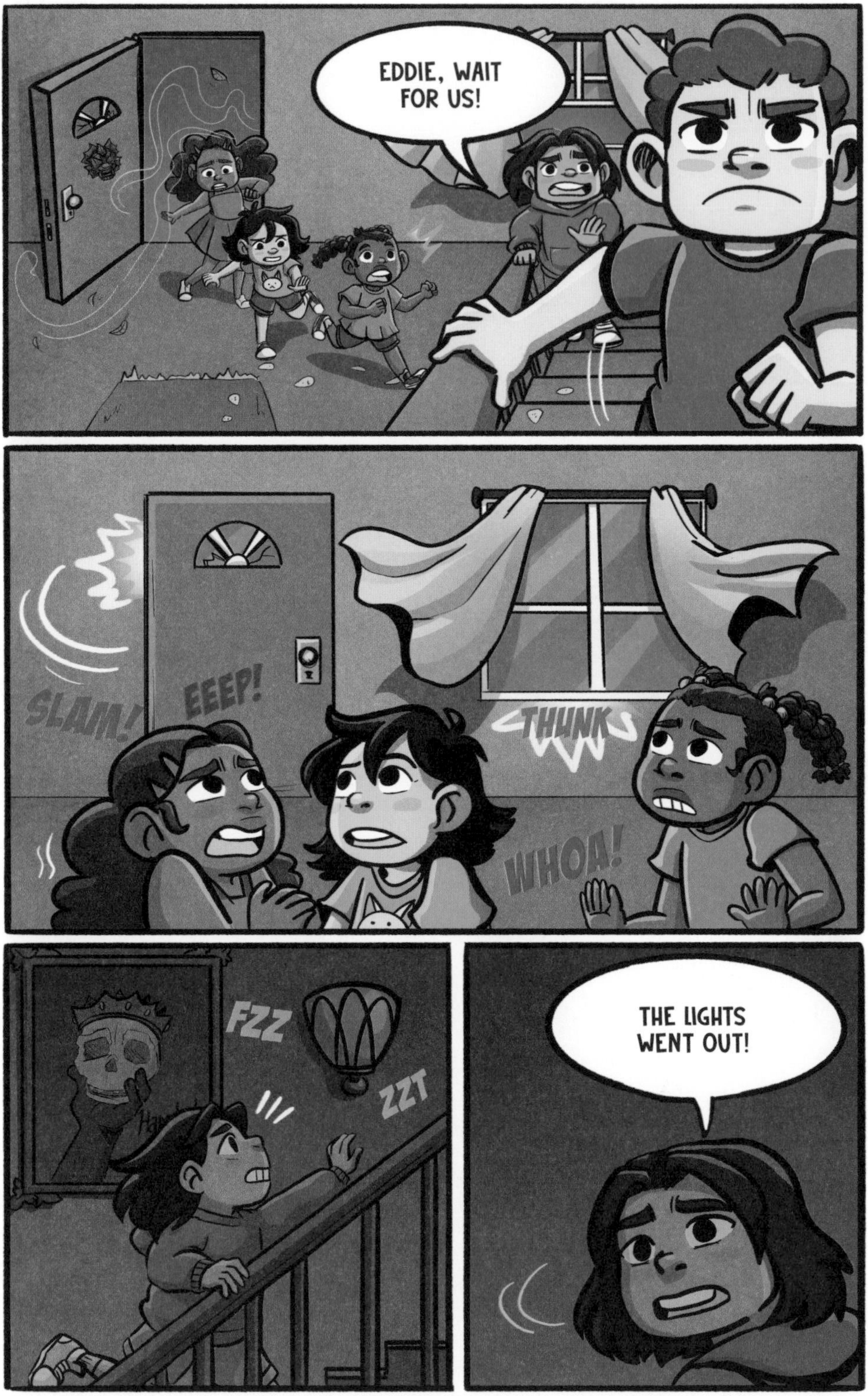
EDDIE, WAIT FOR US!
SLAM!
EEEP!
THUNK
WHOA!
FZZ
ZZT
THE LIGHTS WENT OUT!

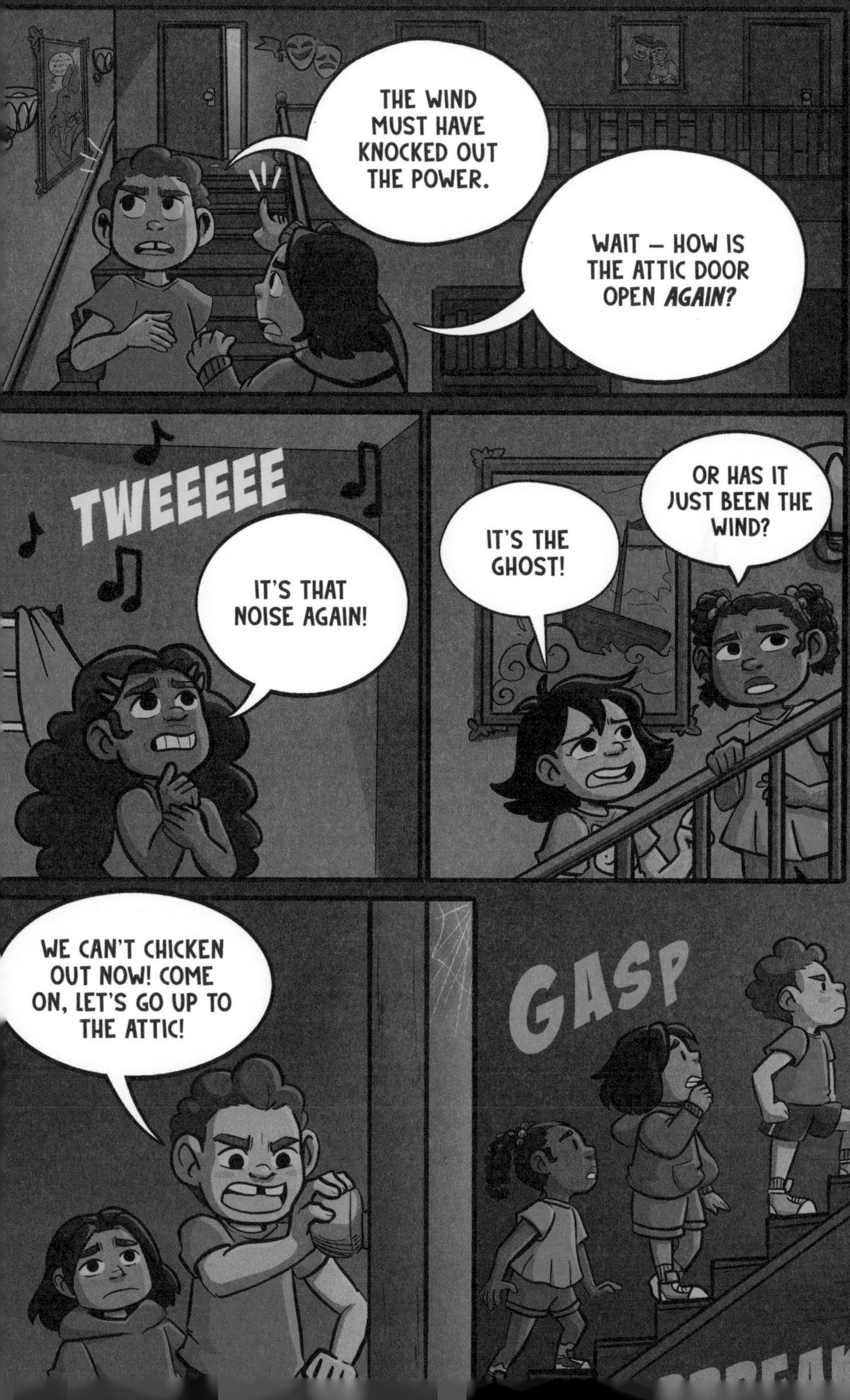
THE WIND MUST HAVE KNOCKED OUT THE POWER.
WAIT — HOW IS THE ATTIC DOOR OPEN *AGAIN?*
TWEEEEE
IT'S THAT NOISE AGAIN!
IT'S THE GHOST!
OR HAS IT JUST BEEN THE WIND?
WE CAN'T CHICKEN OUT NOW! COME ON, LET'S GO UP TO THE ATTIC!
GASP

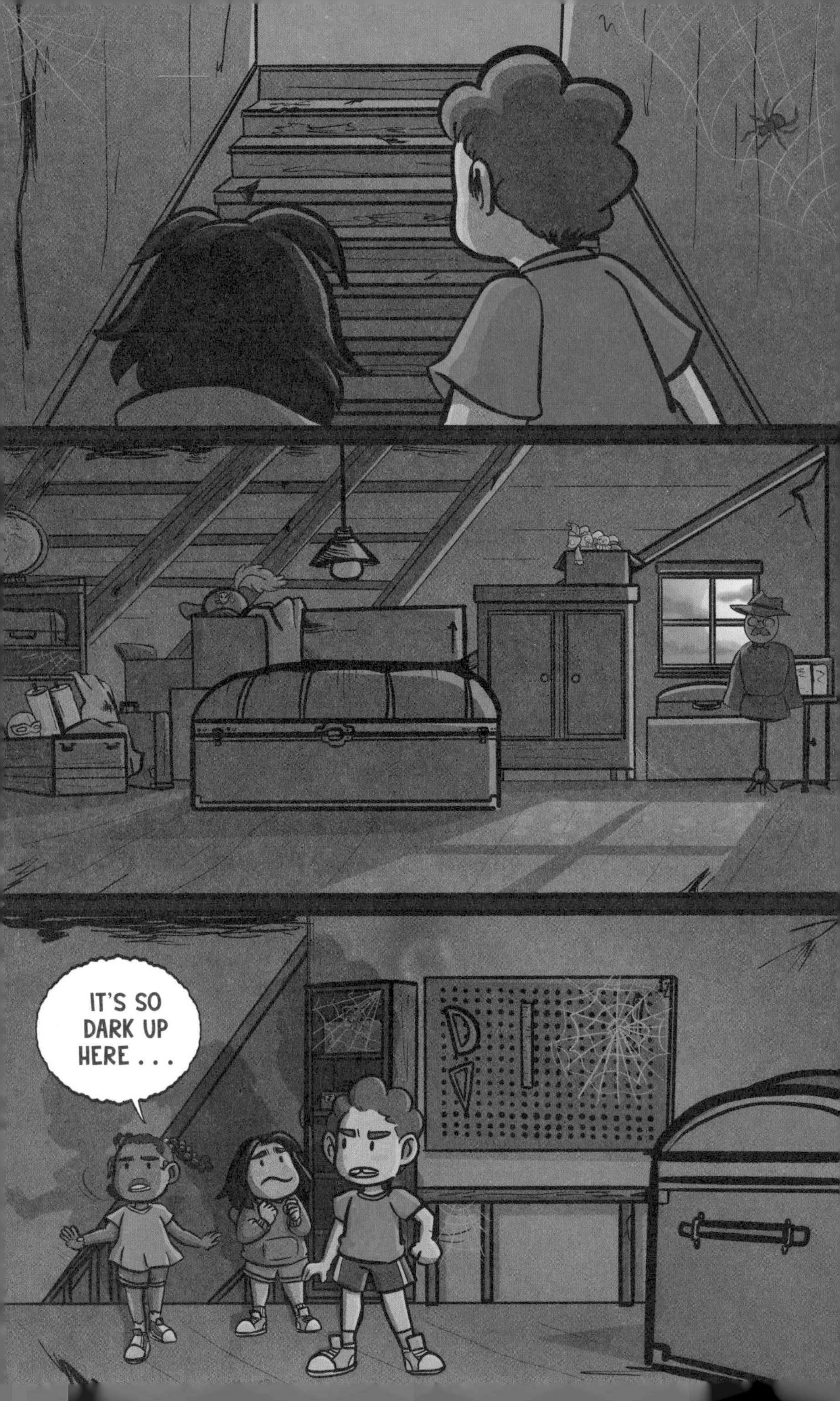
IT'S SO DARK UP HERE . . .

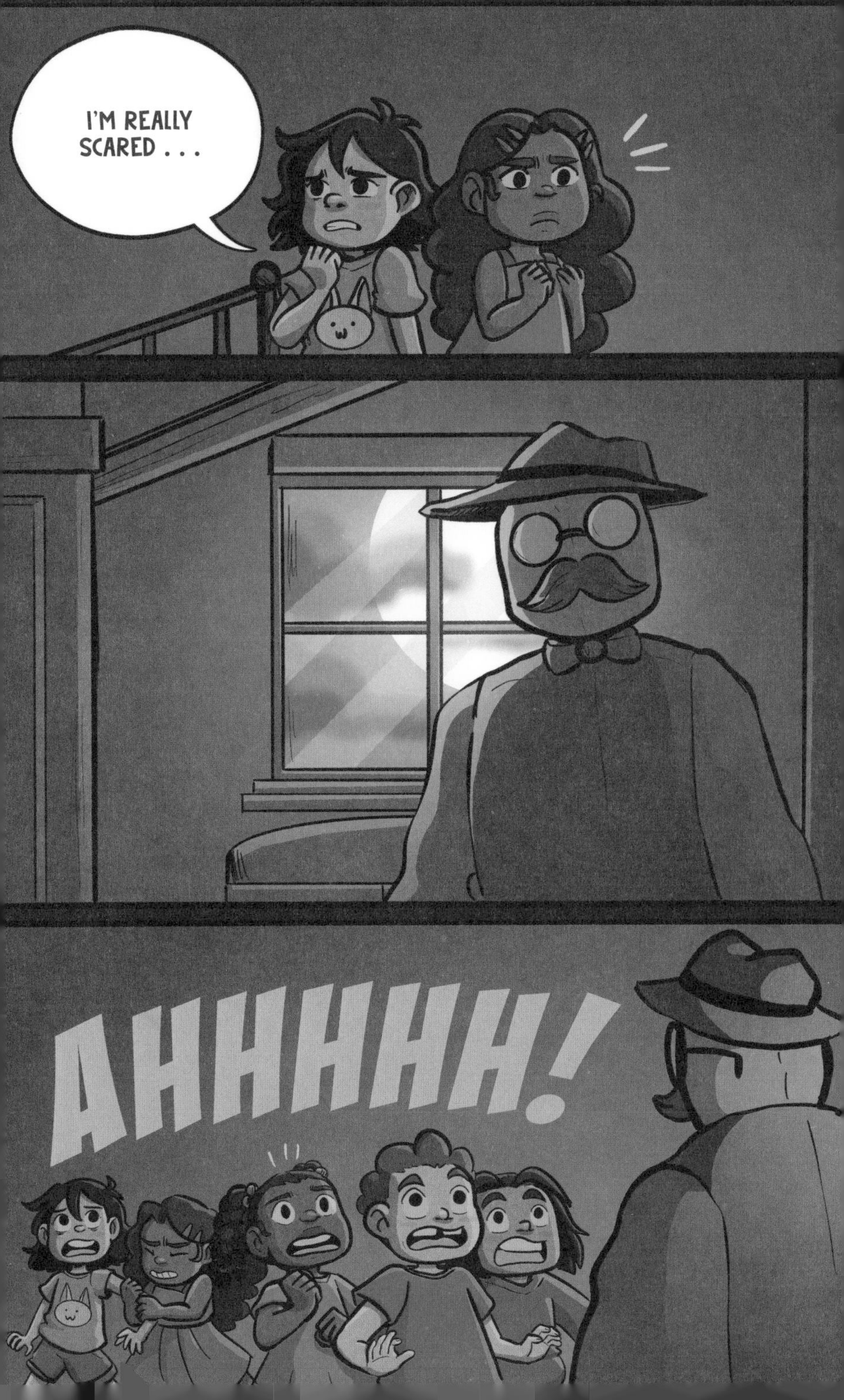
I'M REALLY SCARED . . .
AHHHHH!

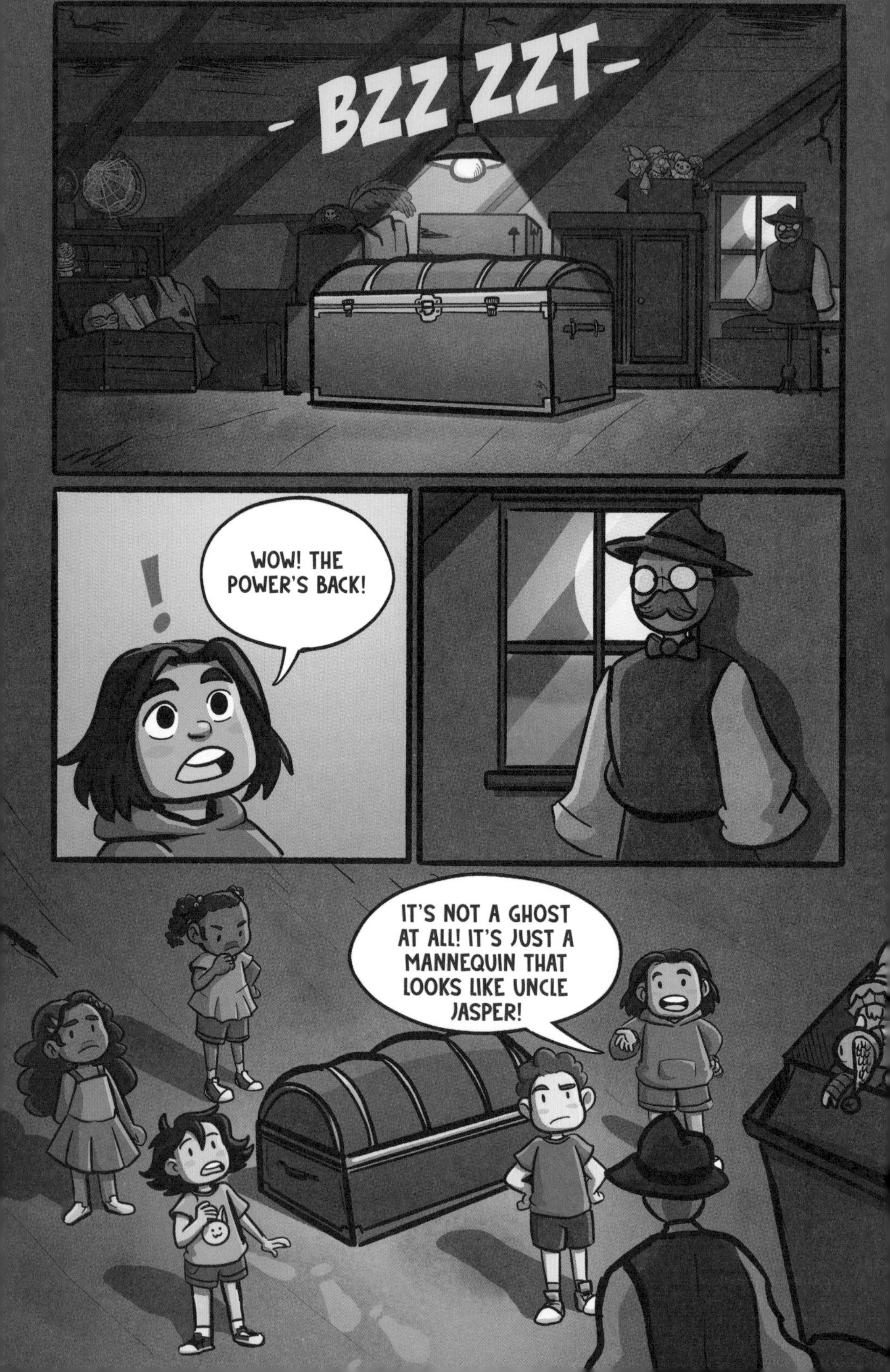
BZZ ZZT
!
WOW! THE POWER'S BACK!
IT'S NOT A GHOST AT ALL! IT'S JUST A MANNEQUIN THAT LOOKS LIKE UNCLE JASPER!

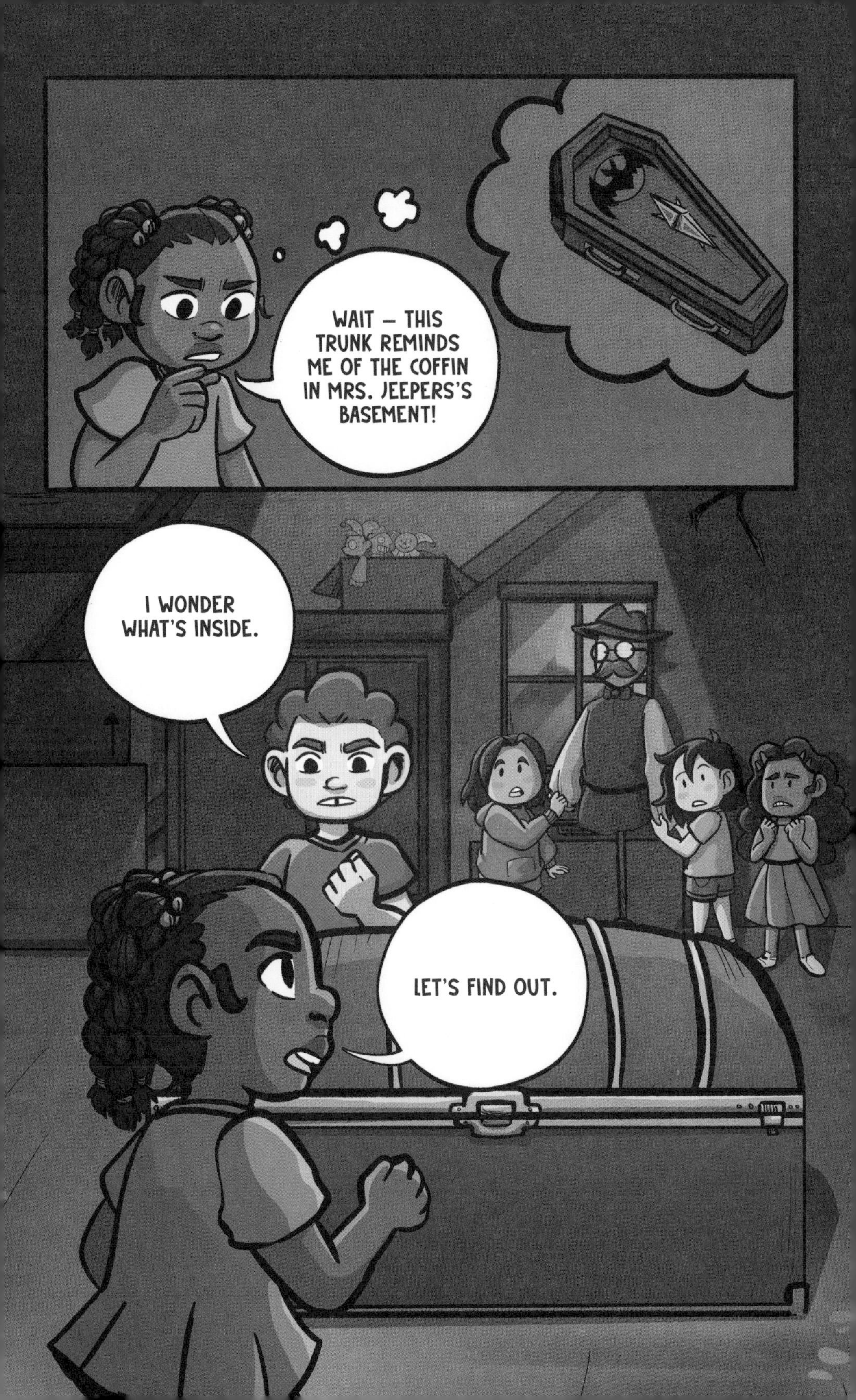
WAIT — THIS TRUNK REMINDS ME OF THE COFFIN IN MRS. JEEPERS'S BASEMENT!
I WONDER WHAT'S INSIDE.
LET'S FIND OUT.

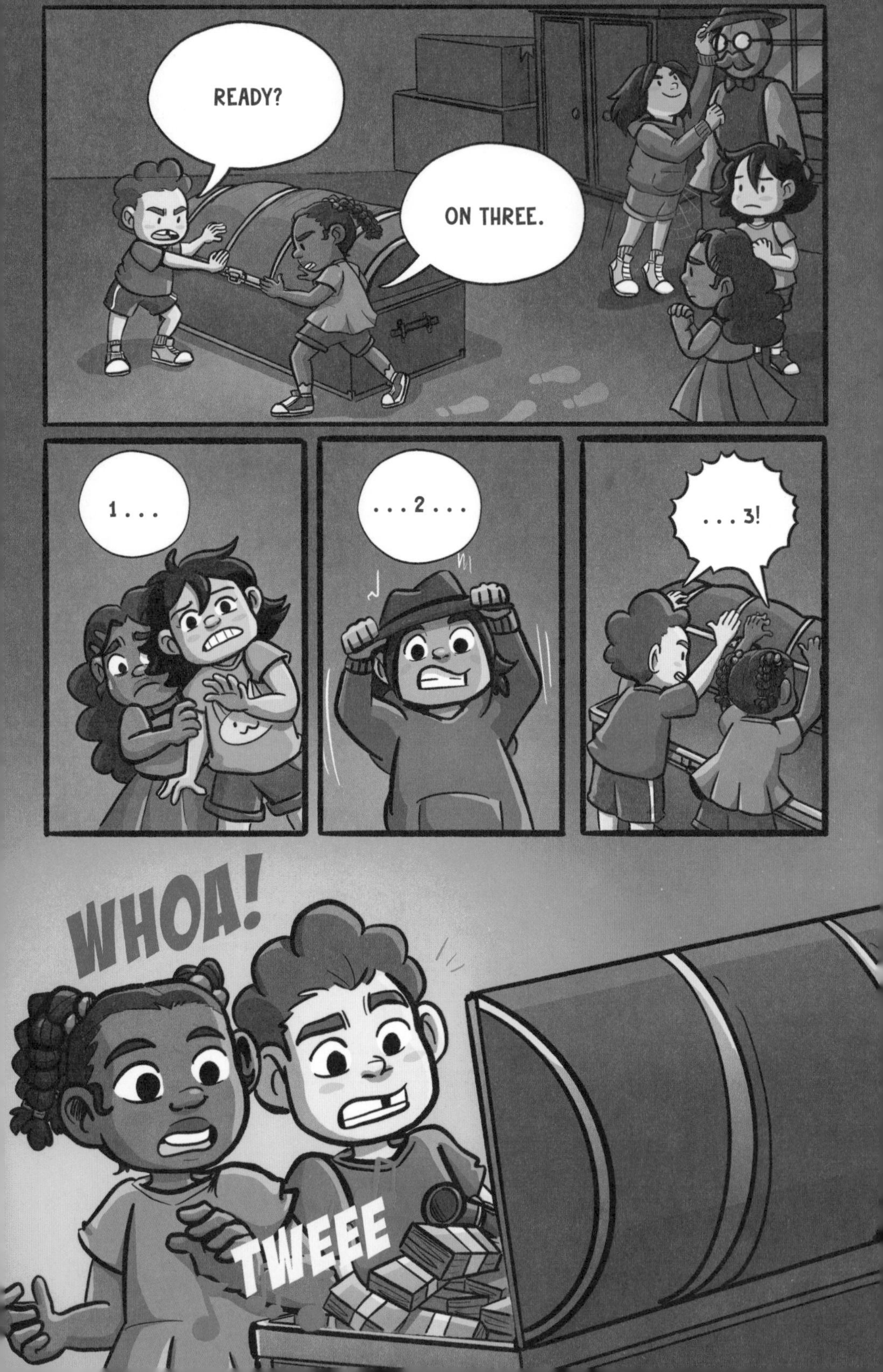
READY?
ON THREE.
1 . . .
. . . 2 . . .
. . . 3!
WHOA!
TWEEE

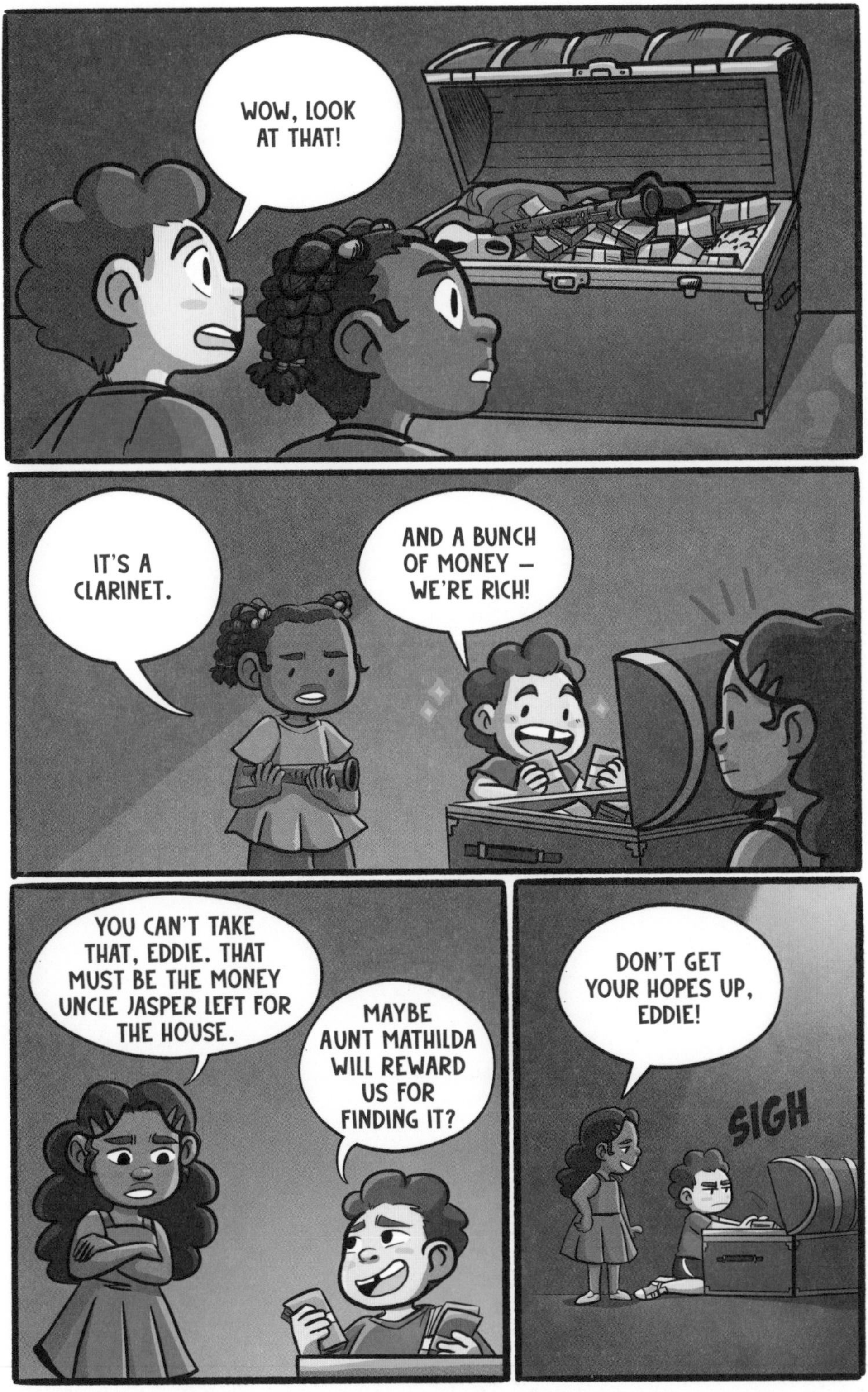
WOW, LOOK AT THAT!
IT'S A CLARINET.
AND A BUNCH OF MONEY — WE'RE RICH!
YOU CAN'T TAKE THAT, EDDIE. THAT MUST BE THE MONEY UNCLE JASPER LEFT FOR THE HOUSE.
MAYBE AUNT MATHILDA WILL REWARD US FOR FINDING IT?
DON'T GET YOUR HOPES UP, EDDIE!
SIGH

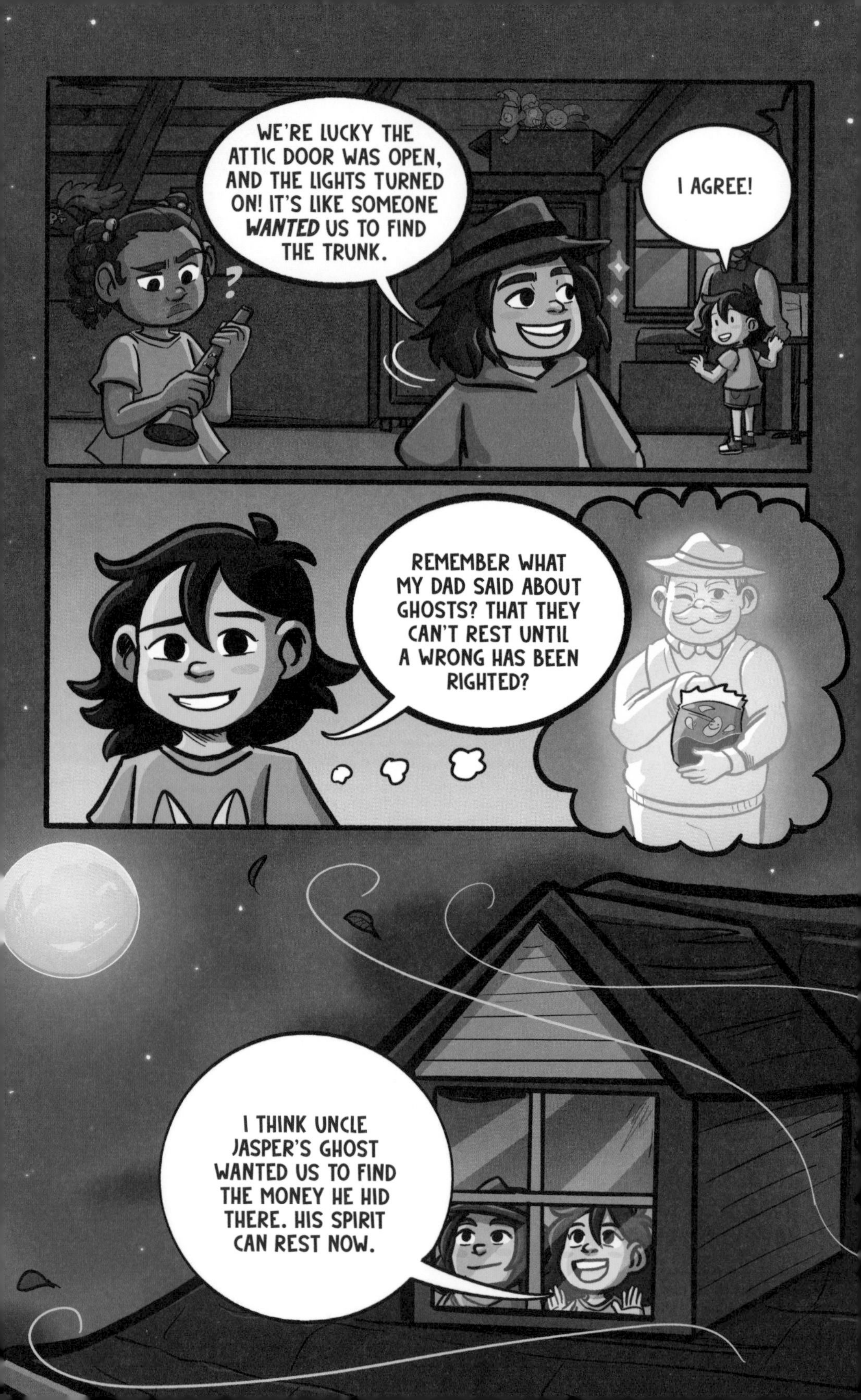
WE'RE LUCKY THE ATTIC DOOR WAS OPEN, AND THE LIGHTS TURNED ON! IT'S LIKE SOMEONE *WANTED* US TO FIND THE TRUNK.
I AGREE!
REMEMBER WHAT MY DAD SAID ABOUT GHOSTS? THAT THEY CAN'T REST UNTIL A WRONG HAS BEEN RIGHTED?
I THINK UNCLE JASPER'S GHOST WANTED US TO FIND THE MONEY HE HID THERE. HIS SPIRIT CAN REST NOW.

CHAPTER 5 WHO ATE THE CHIPS?

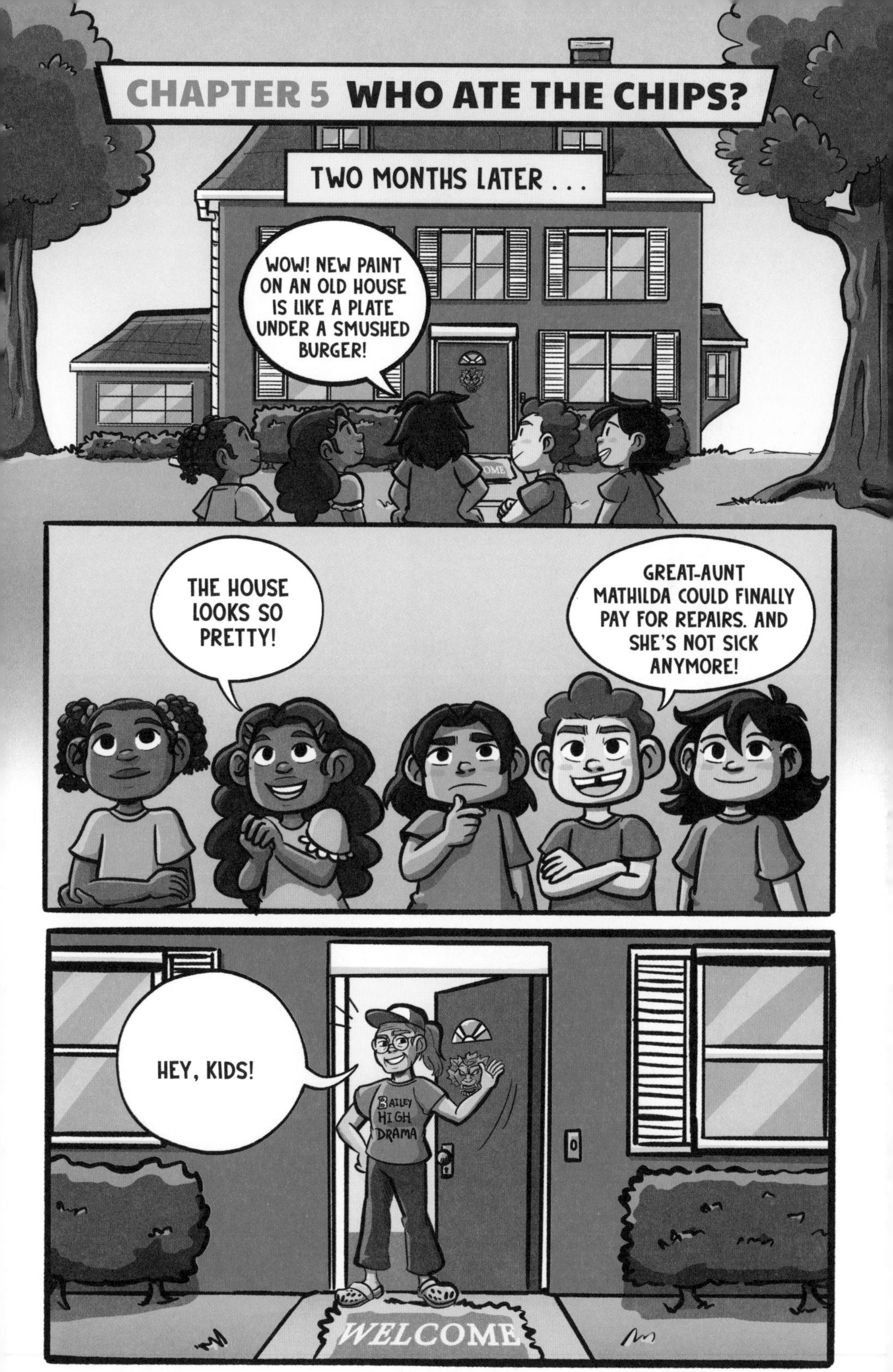
TWO MONTHS LATER . . .
WOW! NEW PAINT ON AN OLD HOUSE IS LIKE A PLATE UNDER A SMUSHED BURGER!
THE HOUSE LOOKS SO PRETTY!
GREAT-AUNT MATHILDA COULD FINALLY PAY FOR REPAIRS. AND SHE'S NOT SICK ANYMORE!
HEY, KIDS!
BAILEY HIGH DRAMA
WELCOME

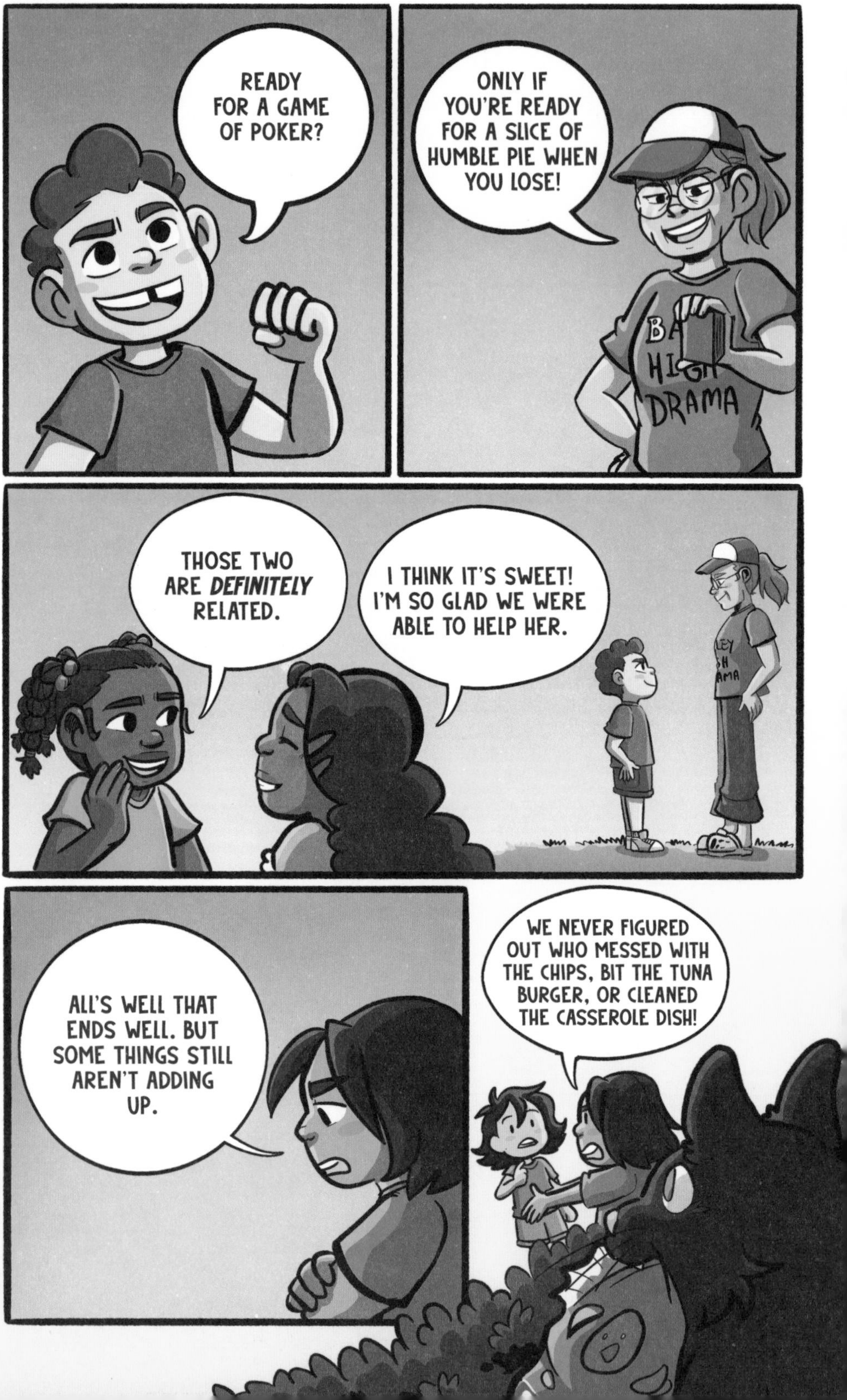
READY FOR A GAME OF POKER?
ONLY IF YOU'RE READY FOR A SLICE OF HUMBLE PIE WHEN YOU LOSE!
DRAMA
THOSE TWO ARE *DEFINITELY* RELATED.
I THINK IT'S SWEET! I'M SO GLAD WE WERE ABLE TO HELP HER.
ALL'S WELL THAT ENDS WELL. BUT SOME THINGS STILL AREN'T ADDING UP.
WE NEVER FIGURED OUT WHO MESSED WITH THE CHIPS, BIT THE TUNA BURGER, OR CLEANED THE CASSEROLE DISH!

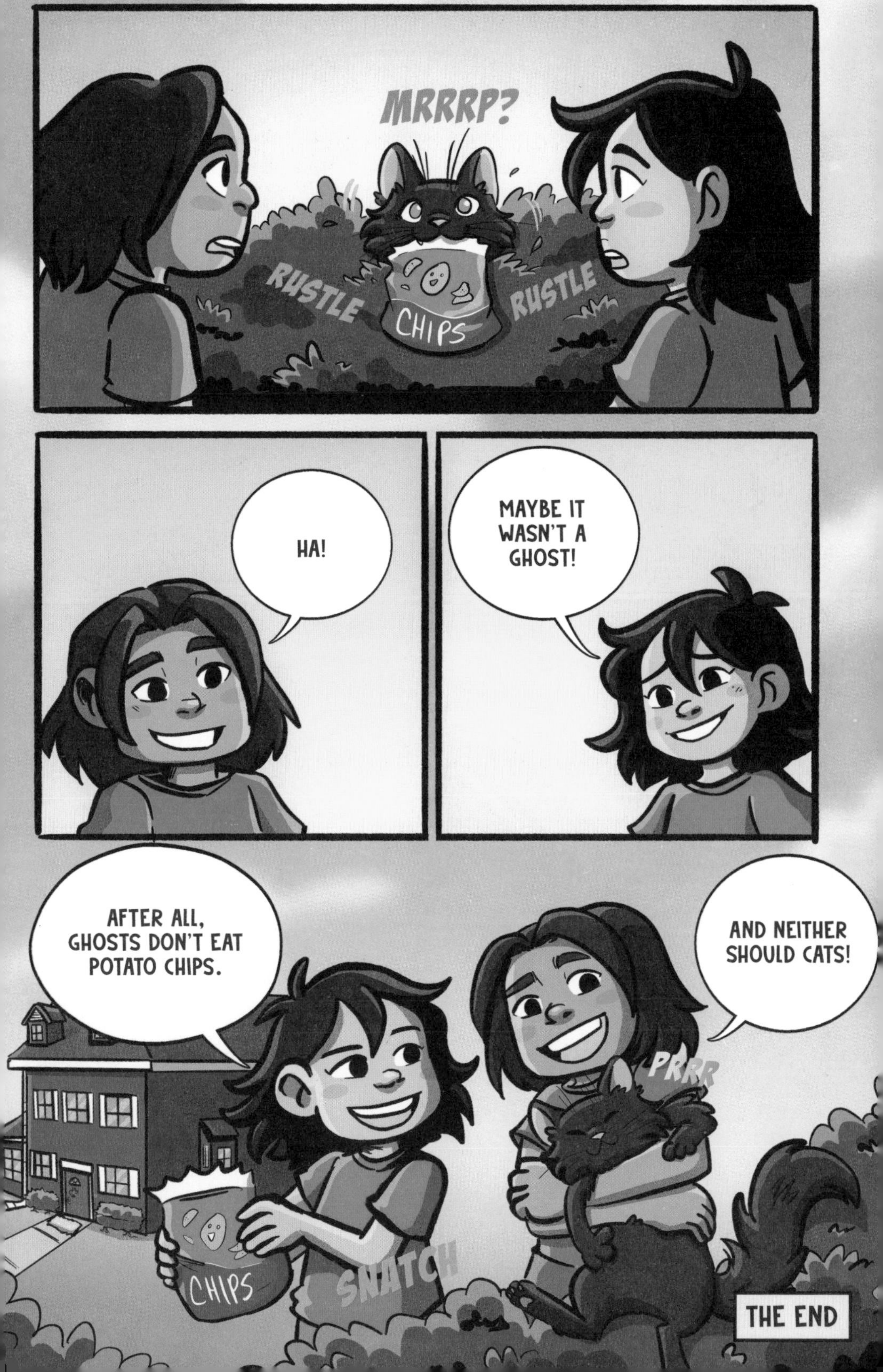
MRRRP?
RUSTLE
CHIPS
RUSTLE
HA!
MAYBE IT WASN'T A GHOST!
AFTER ALL, GHOSTS DON'T EAT POTATO CHIPS.
AND NEITHER SHOULD CATS!
PRRR
CHIPS
SNATCH
THE END

MARCIA THORNTON JONES is an award-winning author who has published more than 130 books for children, including the Adventures of the Bailey School Kids series, *Woodford Brave, Ratfink,* and *Champ.* Marcia lives with her husband, Steve, and two cats in Lexington, Kentucky, where she continues to write, mentor writers, and teach writing classes. She is the coordinator of the Carnegie Center Author Academy, an intensive one-on-one writing program for adult writers working toward publication.

DEBBIE DADEY grew up in Kentucky and now lives in a log cabin in Tennessee with her husband and two greyhound rescues. Her three adult children continue to inspire her. A former first-grade teacher and school librarian, she is the author and coauthor of 182 books, including the Adventures of the Bailey School Kids series. Her newest series, Mini Mermaid Tales, is a multicultural easy chapter book series from Simon and Schuster. Her newest picture book is *Never Give Up: Dr. Kati Karikó and the Race for the Future of Vaccines.*

ANGELI RAFER is a Filipino American illustrator and comic artist based in the diner capital of the world (a.k.a. New Jersey). She is a self-taught digital artist, with a passion for telling stories about everyday magic — from cooking and first crushes to cute animals and bad puns. Her work also appears in several anthologies: Hellcat Press's *Screams Heard Round the World*, *Dark Lady Returns*, and the Sequential Artist Workshop's *Rhythms.*